OLIWIA

By Marco Dias

Published in Great Britain by
L.R. Price Publications Ltd, 2021
27 Old Gloucester Street,
London, WC1N 3AX
www.lrpricepublications.com

ISBN: 9781838339531

DEDICATION

This book is dedicated to my father, the God and Devil in me, the man that laid the foundations of who I am today. Thank you, Father! Thanks to you I know what love and hate are and what I can do with it. I know also that you are still with us somewhere and that if you had to leave us so soon it can only be because you were needed in Heaven, Hell or somewhere else. The writing process is an amazing experience because when we put our hands on a keyboard and start writing a story, sometimes what we thought we wanted to say at the beginning is now an old story. I like stories. I like reading stories. The magic of being a writer is that we can create our own stories and then read it and say I like or I don't like. I like this one. I think it's a brilliant story. Take a break from the real world and come with me to the other world.

.

Marco Dias

OLIWIA

If I could only go back to be a primate, all my troubles would be over and I would once again fear the darkest places without the need of a light called reason and Love would then have meaning. Maybe then, alone in that emptiness I could feel free again and my heart and my eyes would never know what crying means. If I could only be there in the beginning of all things, I would stop evolution and our feelings would never turn into pain and no one would come in between this that we have printed in our souls. But I don't have any superhuman gifts and I cannot make time implode (yet). Maybe one day I can transform light into darkness and cover us with it and then, in that place, hidden from opinion and reasoning, perhaps then we could find peace in each other's arms. – Ah! – And then everything would be silent and there would be no need for words or judgments, there would not be anything left to be said because words would not belong in such a classic painting. There, in that vacuum free of conventions, we would be the only critics of the art we are together. But I'm not a superhero, and evolution cannot be stopped the same way our love should not be restrained. If I could only go back to not to be, back to the moment you first looked at me, I would close my eyes so I could not see and then maybe we could both be truly happy. But I cannot undo what fate united, and so here we are agonising, for all wishes can't be ours and here I'm standing still, looking at the clouds, counting minutes that turn into hours, hours that become days, days evolving into weeks… imprisoned in a world full of freaks where Love is but a black dove of pricks. – Ah! If I could only turn the world upside down and shake away those who don't want us together, only then we could love forever. If only you and me could be what we are meant to be! Like the birds following the calling of migrations or the clouds moving eternally slowly in the skies, going quietly somewhere, minding only the rules of physics… If only you and I could belong like berries in their bushes and the Japanese with their sushi… If only I and you could be added up making two…

M. P.S.D.

CHAPTER 1

Epiphany

I remember well the Sundays at church when I was a little boy. That was a special day for me. There was something magical and transcendental with all the rituals and emotions that took place before, during and after I went to church with my parents and grandparents. Something would take me to a place in the Dark Ages, a place where there was only one word that made everything have sense and that made also life a simple place to live. God. In those days running water was not a common thing yet in many houses in my village. There was always food on my plate three times a day and I had plenty of clothes to dress and even new clothes only for Sunday. I think that at that time I could say I wasn't poor or middle class; I could classify myself something in between that. Sunday, early morning, meant a hot water bath either at my parents' or at my grandparents'. I preferred when my grandmother did it. She would boil a huge 30 litres pan of water in the kitchen – the same used to do stews when all the family got together on special occasions like birthdays, Easter, Christmas and so on – and then she would bath me inside an even bigger round plastic recipient like a round Tupperware used by giants. I can see clearly that huge wine cellar room (24 by 18 feet) in my mind. The black earth floor, hard as rock due to ages of use. The high celling, displaying the old roof tiles resting on long eucalyptus bars crossed with smaller ones, revealing here and there bright beams of light illuminating the room as the sun baths the planet Earth with energy. Everywhere there were dusty and old spider webs tunnelling towards the cracks in the walls and to the wooden bars. Huge stacks of hay (for feeding the cows, pigs, goats, sheep and rabbits living in other rooms nearby) piled against another wall. Old wooden chests filled with salted meat and small agriculture utensils, different kinds of shovels, forks, rake and scythes hanging on the walls. There was up to a dozen of wine barrels against a wall going from the size of a car tyre to the size of harvester farm tractor water tyres. Many other things can be found in there. All that created a melting pot of scents: the soil and the wine and its vinegar and sulphur odour; the smell of the potatoes on the ground in the corner; the smell of aged oak chests and barrels and the pong of the salted meats. All those artefacts and fragrances united together created the most magical bathroom. My grandmother would then lay on the floor an old blanket underneath the round tub maybe to make it a warmer and cosy place. I would stand there naked in the middle of the bath waiting for her to temper the boiling water that she would use after to wash me. My job was easy. I just needed to stay peacefully whilst she would prewash all my body in a very diligent manner with water and soap. It was a funny moment for both of us. We would laugh. And she would talk me through all the steps of how to wash my body in the future: scrub your hair; wash behind and inside ears; my armpits; my ass; my willy and finally my feet. In the end she would smile at me, wrap me in a towel and carry me to the room where my best clothes would be waiting for me. She would then dress and tidy me like an angel, and on that day I was not allowed to go play in the patio outside. I loved to sleep over at theirs. There is something quite magical and free when we are with our grandparents. Maybe it's just because they feel they have a second chance of educating someone and they see it as a way of doing better. After they would get ready as well and all of us would then wait in silence in the kitchen or at the living room for my parents to arrive and take all of us by car to the church at the city nearby. To some degree going to church was like being with God or Jesus in flesh. The conversations were minimal and all of them were already focused on what would happen very soon: the gathering of people by the high and wide staircase in front of the house of God; the moment everyone would sin as much as they could because very soon redemption was coming again inside through prayer and confession. They would compare the means of transportation, what people were wearing, the hair, the moustache, the jewellery and even the way they talked, more or less colloquial and so on. Most of that moment was whispered, so I'm not sure what they were talking about. I felt it was only rubbish and many of the seven capital sins were being displayed there, in front of me and the house of our Lord. Well, that's how I saw it and hear it, but I'm not sure if I was right because I was only six and people tend to say that children still have a lot to learn before they can emit clever opinions about any subject (and how often wrong adults are). My dad or my grandfather would usually put me on their lap so I wouldn't get lost in the crowd of believers or kidnapped by some God-devoted paedophile soul (a common attendant of these places) – I thought. I remember looking at the immense building with a couple of two high-arched doors decorated with the most exquisite handmade thick wood, finished with even more amazing stained-glass murals with ecclesiastical motifs. It was over-whelming and I recall thinking how tall God, Jesus and all saints must have been. They were giants for sure. And then the moment to go inside arrived. Like good Christians everyone pushed themselves in silence forcing the way in a chaotic but Christian manner, like a herd of mammals, in order to sit as close as they could to the messenger of God – for me a funny-looking man dressed like a woman with a Klu Klux Klan hat on his head and a couple of others dressed in funny white dress holding either tall candles or prophetic books. This part of the church ostentation I never really understood because my family always told me how simple Jesus was. Maybe Jesus had asked them to dress like that. I'm sure that was the reason and because he was so poor all his life, that has to be also the reason why cathedrals had to be so big and show so much richness. It had to be. It makes sense. My dad never hurried to go in-side. He always knew there was a seat for all of us, some-where inside that huge place. For him even if he had to stand by the last row of seats of that Stratolaunch (an air-craft much bigger than the A380), he would still sense peace and feel that he was a good Christian. He only worried about doing the sign of the cross from his head to his chest and then from his right shoulder finishing it on his left shoulder and to step in with his right foot. Until I was explained the reason why people do the sign of the cross, I always thought that he was shaking flies away, or something like that, every time he did it. To be honest I was just there to eat the bread and ask my dad for coins for the common alms that took place near the end of the mass. I guess that I was never easily entranced by the colours, scents and images displayed inside that magical place and at the time I didn't fancy theatre plays that much. People would repeat prayers and sentences coming out of the black book and hug and kiss and smile like they loved each other. I knew I was just a small boy and that I didn't know much about life, but somehow something was not right in that picture. Maybe in order to be a good Christian you need to go to acting school – I thought. Whatever was going on in there no doubt people believed in it. And what is religion if not just that, a crazy belief in something that you can't touch but that fills your heart with hope? Like I said I was just a kid and for me I supposed it was not fair that only the man in the girly funny dress had all the bread and was the only one getting drunk.

As time went by and I grew older, I guess, people, just like I did, stopped going to the theatres, maybe because they hadn't enough money to pay for the plays or perhaps they started getting bored of watching the same scene time after time; whatever it was, ten years after, my family stopped going there. They would still read texts from the same strange black book and chant prayers every night, but it was as if they had managed to get out of that middle-age trance that any church represents. For me nothing changed much. There was always fresh bread in my house; whenever I needed coins, I would still ask for them from my dad and by then I was already allowed to have my own glass of wine.

For this story it doesn't really matter the reasons why I came from Portugal to live in this amazing country called England (maybe because you helped us to defeat Napoleon Bonaparte in what would stay in history as perhaps the first war alliance between two countries) or why I chose Brighton as my favourite city to live, or with whom I came into this country, or who those people are or where they are now; that is matter for many other stories that have nothing to do with the 13th of March of 2015. Only this day has a transcending meaning. Many times in life things happen to me – maybe with everyone – that go past the rational understanding of any human being. Now and again if we pay attention to some hidden signs in our dreams and to our deepest feelings and to the connections we have with people and things in this world, we will comprehend why science can't explain everything and why religion and faith have still a major role in society. You know what I'm talking about? Déjà vu experiences, visions with secret messages, gut feelings, premonitions, near death experiences, magic and many other familiarities that belong only in the realm of the unsolved. I had a few in my life and I'm sure many of you had it also. We all do. The difference lies, often, in those who can read between the lines or in those that are willing to embrace mystery. I can say on my behalf that the reason why I have to embrace mystery is because during my life I experienced many unexplainable incidents and also because I had the opportunity and the will to read many books about all sorts of subjects and see hundreds of documentaries and movies covering all themes starting on Earth and finishing at the unknown; I studied the cells and the dinosaurs and all the elements of the periodic table and so on, but more important than that, I had the chance to meet many humans like me from the age of one to the age of one hundred and people from all races and creeds and different demography. We have all something special within. It's a fact and we shouldn't waste our lives pretending we don't matter, because we do, and we all have a role to play in this universe; primarily it's life and the will to live and thrive in this tiny ball called Earth. More than any isms and evolution I trust that faith (and we can all have a different one) is the key to either destroy our society or unite it in peace. Because I'm an optimist by nature I choose the second option. In the end life is very simple. Everyone knows it and everybody has heard about it somewhere or put their eyes on sentences like this: we collect what we sowed; tell me with whom you hang out and I'll tell you who you are; karma and fate. How many of you thought about bad outcomes for your life and you got it? On the other hand, when you are genuinely good and spread love around you, how many of you had true and honest smiles and feelings and good gestures coming back to you? Life is an easy place – we just complicated it too much, right? My father would say this to me with a bright and hopeful smile on his face and then he would take me by his hand and show me the animals inside the shed or would walk with me the narrow path leading to his crops in the land behind our house. He was very proud of that and he loved me very much.

March 11th 2015 – *from a dream to reality*

I had a normal of work, had been writing since early morning; an ordinary shower, a usual dinner and then I read a bit from my *Kafka by the shore* by Haruki Murakami and went to sleep around 0:00. The 13th of March of 2015 had started. When it comes to sleep, I'm like the dogs. I always start with what it feels being the right position for sleeping but then I turn and turn again 20 times in bed, ending up being comfortable exactly in the same place I was in the beginning. I guess that's the animal instinct in me. Something many people say humans don't have and only creatures do; instinct. Well, I don't agree with that just for the simple reason that that is what I am in the end – an instinctive being. Everyone knows that we dream every night; even when we say we don't we actually do. People just can't remember it all the time, but I will leave that for someone else like you to discover the reasons why. This night, however, I would remember every detail of my dream. I remember being at the kitchen of my shared house in Brighton. I had been sitting at my kitchen table with my notebook in front of me, but I wasn't writing. I had my iPhone connected by Bluetooth to my portable speaker and I was listening to Japanese instrumental Trip-Hop and going through the inspiring works of Picasso inside an Essential Picasso book I like to carry around with me. But something wasn't right: I could feel my blood boiling gently in all my veins. I must have gotten out of that chair and walked outside to the patio or to my room at least half a dozen times. You know how birds and animals get distressed before storms and earthquakes? That's exactly how I was feeling. I sat down again on the chair and kept looking at Picasso's works. I was looking at his work called *The Muse* from 1935 when one of my mates living in that house (and it doesn't matter who he is – not for this book) said hello and I replied hello back. He asked me what I was up to with a smile on his face. It took me a few seconds answering and after I said, now looking at *Guernica*, that I wasn't quite sure, but I was feeling bored and upset. I followed by telling him that it was such a beautiful evening – it was sunny and quite warm for March in Brighton – and that I was thinking of going to the seafront and down to the beach to watch the sunset to relax my mind a bit and asked him if he would like to go with me – and let's make clear that I respect all sexual orientations but I'm not a fairy from the south. I was feeling a bit lonely and felt I needed someone to talk to. He then answered that it was OK with him but firstly he would prepare dinner for himself, and if I wanted, he would share it   with me.

I thought about it and said, 'OK, it's fine, I'll stay here with you and then we go together.'

He started then preparing the food and I guess that less than a minute after I jumped out of the chair and told him, 'Listen, I need to go now, OK?'

He was a bit surprised and said it was fine, but he would stay and maybe he would join me after. He added something like: 'What's going on, M., do you have a date or something?' and gave me a cheeky smile.

I smiled back to him and explained that something was calling me outside. I did not know what it was, but I had to go now, and so I did. He looked at me as if I was crazy and when I was leaving just before I closed the door behind me I told him that I was going to find myself a princess – I don't know why, but that's exactly what I said. 'I'm going to find myself a princess,' and I left carrying this relaxed and amazing thought in my mind, 'I'm going to find myself a princess.'

I left Rugby Place and took the narrow alley that leads to Whitehawk Road and from there it's five minutes to get to the seafront. I like to go there and sit down by the sea close to the marina. It's quite relaxing there, away from the confusing and sometimes overpopulated world of Brighton that starts a couple of miles away, where the new slide would be built in a couple of years, not until after the statue of the Angel of Freedom. I love the beauty of thousands of people together but often I prefer to be alone with my buttons. Again, even being a human, I'm very much like the animals with my habits. This said, once I got to the sidewalk by the wall, after crossing Marine Parade or A259 to the other side – whichever you want to call it – when in there by the wall I would always do the same: I breathe in deeply the breeze pushed by the wind from the sea and look at the view towards France. Sometimes I bother counting the windmills at the wind farm a few miles away in the sea and then I looked at the pier down in Brighton; look for a few seconds to the 360 eye until I understand if it's going up or down, and after I look at the marina and at the path that goes along the sea to Saltdean and finally I put my eyes on my spot, the place I like to sit, my cradle. If it's available – and usually it is – I smile and if it's not, I wonder why someone had to pick that specific place to sit and end up sitting down close by. It was now 17:45. I could see the sun a few inches away from touching the horizon line. There was no one in my place. I smiled and looked at the sky – made now of long brushes of light blue, orange and pink; no white brushes of planes crossing the skies in that moment – I closed my eyes for a brief second and breathed deeply again but when I opened my eyes and looked at my spot I could now see what seemed the shape of a woman sitting down facing the sea, and it looked as if she was also reading a book or writing or something like that. Don't you just love dreams? My heart started working fast like a little sparrow. I looked at my watch and it was now 17:47. Like when we drive a car entranced with our thoughts and get to places without recalling driving there, by 17:51 I was sitting one hand away from her. She had closed her book and oh, my God, how beautiful she was! We both smiled at each other in peace and decided to hold hands facing south watching the sun disappear behind the pier. It felt like we both joined together in a descending count until the moment the sun gave place to dawn; 5. 4. 3. 2. 1. 0. Five seconds that touched me like an eternity. I felt so relaxed and at peace. It stroked me as if I had been touched by an angel. After she let my hand go, she carried on reading her book. There was nothing wrong with that. I closed my eyes and turned my face to the sky and inspired my lungs profoundly again and then looked to her and she was still there. I don't know how long we sat together but during that time I watched her beauty and all her expressions. I could try describing her beauty, but how can we define the beauty of an angel? Let's say she looked like Lara Croft in her 20s when she used a ponytail but dressed smart with blue jeans and an immaculate white shirt under an army green-coloured Timberland jacket. She was wearing white all-stars without socks and I'll say no more. I stayed in silence with her for an undetermined time frame (the unexplained freedom of time during dreams). I could see by the density of the book she was reading that it should have around 250 pages and she had probably read around the first 50. She never looked at me during that time. I could see her smiling with some passages and now and then her face would dive into the sad expressions. I respected her, I think. I wished I could use that time with her to know her better, but if a woman wants to be alone, we need to respect that. The same way they will tell us when they need and want our attention – I think. So, I kept my guard low and indulged my heart with that angelical moment. At some point of that dream something, some sort of unwelcome interference came to shake that perfect instant like a quake shakes life's serenity away, transforming happiness into chaos in a blink. You know, like in that movie *Ghost in a Shell* with Scarlet Johansson when at some moments she starts seeing images of her past showing up in places where it did not belong? Like the image of a Chinese temple screening up in front of you inside your local Costa, a touch completely odd that doesn't belong in such an idyllic place? You understand what I'm talking about, right? That's what materialised with my dream. At first it signalled like music coming from the distance. But it wasn't music, it was something else. She felt it and heard it too, just like me, and she closed her book. We both knew that our moment was about to end. I felt that she wanted to give an important message; a transcending meaning for why we had met there. Everything in life happens for a reason; usually we are to blame for our fate, but not so often things happen inexplicably. The interference in my dream started diluting the dream away. Our shapes and the shapes surrounding us were fading away like a lantern losing battery. That sound was closer and closer to us now. She laid her book on her lap and turned straight to me with her arms wide open and smiled. I could see her book on her lap. The hard cover was completely white. That book had no name. The sound we were listening to disturbing our dream that seemed like a song at first had now become the ring tone of my iPhone. My device had been ringing non-stop for I don't know how long, and the interference was now unbearable. As if both of us got caught in a twisting tornado we hugged like a mother would hug her child just before burying him or like Romeo and Juliet would hug before killing themselves. Before that dream was over, whilst we were vanishing inside that tornado and in a close strong and peaceful hug I whispered into her ear: 'May I know your name?'

And she whispered back to me: 'Yes. My name is Oliwia.'

And the dream was over. In a flash I was brought back to my room in Brighton and like a lost and uncontrolled spring I jumped out of my bed. My phone was ringing. But I couldn't find my phone. It was there just in front of me. The screen was lit, and I could see it was my mother calling me. It was probably 5:00 am. I was looking at the phone in disbelief. It couldn't be my mother, not at that time, unless something really bad had happened. But everything was fine, so why was she calling me? I even thought of pretending I was sleeping and then I would call her back in the morning excusing myself, saying that I was very tired and that's why I did not hear the call. But I knew I had to take that call. So, somehow, I snapped out of that trance and took the call.

'Hi, Mum. Is everything OK?' I asked.

From the other side of the line a voice in a defeated and lost tone and the image of the Virgin Mary crying by the cross, brushed a Francis Bacon painting in my soul. I had heard a similar desperate tone like that before in my life.

'Son? Son? My son? Son?' She was crying like I never heard or felt in the past. I couldn't say anything for a while. I froze. She knew I was there with her and she cried even more. 'Son? Son?' She couldn't say it and I couldn't ask her. At that point my heart and my soul were invaded by a new feeling. Something I don't wish anyone to feel. Something that only by loving we can explain. I tried to think of an alternative. Maybe it was something bad but not what I thought it was.

So, in a desperate attempt to change fate I told my mother: 'Mum? Mum? What's going on? Mum, what's going on? What's happened?'

She was waiting for this question. She couldn't say anything for the next minute. Uncontrollable despair installed in our souls. I wasn't yet sure of what happened, but I couldn't help myself. Whatever she would have to tell me, she would tell very soon; it didn't matter anymore. I joined her in her pain and cried with her.

'M., my son, it's your father...' and she went silent.

'My father... what happened to my father, Mum?'

She cried even harder. She didn't have anything else to say. I knew it now. She would tell me what I could not swallow, but before she did my mind went on a spiral of memories with him. I went back and forward into those celebrations one thousand times. I saw him holding me tight and protecting me against all dangers, I saw him sad and angry and joyful. He was smiling at me, when from the other side of the phone, the pale voice of my mother kept repeating the same words: 'Your father died in his sleep. M., are you there? They say your father died in his sleep. M., are you there? M., are you there? My husband died! M., are you there?'

I wouldn't be there for the next five minutes. I went on holidays with my father during that time. I don't want to talk about it anymore for now, I hope you don't mind. Later in this story my father will be back. For now, I will recall the last of that fateful March the 13th. My mum's voice stopped making any sense in my mind. I felt I was again back into a dream. In that dream I was sad, but I wasn't crying. In that dream I was sitting down on the edge of my bed in the dark in my house in Brighton. My head was facing the ceiling. Flashes of images of my father and me screened on that celling. I wasn't saying anything, but I could hear a lost, abandoned and distant voice that sounded like mine asking the same question over and over again: 'Father? Father? Father? Father? Father?' It would take long until he answered me.

CHAPTER 2

Mist

Brighton March the 8th 2017

I never accepted my father's death, but with time pain eased. I still carry his memories in my heart and I still love him the same. But I carried my life in a blur of belief and disbelief. Life must go on, so they say. So, I tried to accept that I'm just a human being and that I'm not inexorable as the idea of time is. That was about to change very soon but later on in this story.

And to start that tale I want to say something for those who like me put on weight easily and often feel that even breathing air makes us fat, especially for those, I'll tell something that in the end is not secret: the question about being fat shouldn't even be part of the equation for happiness (unless like in language you have some sort of inability for learning or for your body a hormonal unbalance). Except that, just forget about it. That doesn't really matter. The more I think about rubbish the added layered nonsense I become. I used to know a guy by the name of Don't Matter that was crazy about sports and he was actually a very fit chap. Not really psychologically, but more a kind of a little Forest Gump. He had the potential of a superstar, but he was too troubled to think like a proper one. Don't Matter dreamed as high as the next star in the universe, he was the next habitable planet on the nearest solar system. To a certain degree I think like him when it comes to doing sports and especially about jogging. Running is fundamental for our core muscles and highly relaxing and meditative. Many times, I see strange people walking tall, elegant and confident on the streets and I know that comes from a running diet. I do it and I recommend it at least two times a week in a total of at least 3.5 miles each time. We are different in the end and what works for me won't necessarily work for you. Whatever makes you fit is what works for you. I love running. I run those miles and I only stop where I started. I don't care about the time it takes me to do it, so I don't count the time. I just get out there and do it and then get home tired and sweaty but with a clear mind and after a shower I look and feel like a new man.

One day when I went running from Brighton to Saltdean and back, as I usually do, the most extraordinary thing happened to me and soon enough it would happen to many other people around in this planet. It was a sunny day on that day of March. The temperature was brilliant for the south of England – around 20 degrees, there were no clouds, and the sky was of a baby blue colour. I walked from where I lived, Rugby Place 666 wearing my white and grey Adidas running shoes, my grey and black running shorts and my black sweatshirt. Mr grey without a private jet. Went past Lidl at number 45 Arundel Road – the car park was busy and full as always. Crazy place it is, by the way. What a sausage that business is; non-stop flux of people and goods coming and going out through that entrance, exit and warehouse doors. People, food and money. Tic-tac, tic-tac, tic-tac. I was reaching the intersection of Arundel Road with the A259 and because there was a bit of traffic at that time I usually would cross to the other side through a man-made small gap between the metallic grid that divides the incoming and outgoing circulation from out of Brighton; as I was saying I would cross there and not at the road traffic lights nearby, and that meant that often I would have to stay there for a couple of minutes waiting. But that did not worry me. As soon as I left home, I was already in a contemplative state of mind, so I used those minutes not to stress about traffic flow but to enjoy the view around me but mainly looking at the sky. It fascinates me during the day and infinitely more during the night. However, something in that moment was in fact disturbing my concentration. My inner silence was fighting with all the noises around me and this time it was losing. Seagulls were strangely noisier, and the motors slowed down for a few moments. I looked at the faces of people inside the cars and all of them were looking somewhere behind my back. A stronger, close noise was building up behind me. I could feel a gigantic monster breathing behind my back. The time it took me turning back; that was the time it took it to fly over me. An A380 went over my head at what seemed to me landing distance – half a mile or so. It surprised me at first, but in the end, there was nothing that abnormal about it. When you live in Brighton, Gatwick airport is just about 30 miles away from here. But this one was going to Europe and then one after another, all planes would come and go below 15,000 feet, nearly halfway the limits of the tropo-sphere. It felt that something wasn't right about it but nothing that could relate to a catastrophic event. As I said, it was strange but acceptable. I was sure there was a good reason for that to be happening and very soon everyone would know about it because it would be all over the news. Like Shakespeare, mass media love and feed from a good tragedy. What better than shattering happenings or a *good* war to keep the motors running? However, that day I saw something in the sky that would forever shake my lack of faith. From somewhere above what would very soon be called the *Death Line,* something was dropped from the sky above. It was a very small object that crossed through what seemed at first an air mirror of the atmosphere above. It's actually hard to explain what I saw but imagine when we drop a rock into a lake; as the rock goes through the water it creates a momentary hole that disappears after and creates that round shock wave in the water that vanishes in a few seconds. It's hard to explain. For me the impression I had was that something had just gently made a hole in the atmosphere, without any sort of friction. And to be fair, what troubled me the most was the fact that there was no way the mesosphere or exosphere or thermosphere (whatever comes first or last – was never brilliant with science) could be so close to me. It was just there. More or less the same distance I was running. If I started running now, I would be by the Death Line in about 30 minutes. It's crazy just to think about it. But I know what I saw, and many other people would see it too. Unfortunately for those that unlike me, who kept it as a mystery, and went to tell the world what they had seen, for those hospices came first and most of them just disappeared. Good thing that I had had close experience with schizophrenia in my past and learned the hard way what karma means when you go talk about your or others' personal life with people you don't know well and take as friends. In the end most of them are Judas. But that's a subject for another book. Going back to the moment that small and strange object crossed the Death Line. What I saw behind it made no sense. For a few seconds I saw the sky shake and like a warm hole I was given the sight of the space; the emptiness between stars the void or the vacuum or whatever. But I did not see shiny stars on a blank canvas. I saw only grey. But a shade I had never seen before. Whatever artist had created that new colour had a special gift. Let's call it for now as the God of creation (of new colours). My first reaction was to blink and think that I'm seeing things. It's possible. Our brain can suggest and create a false image very easily. And I'll go back to that moment very soon, but first I would like to give you an example of how our mind can create misleading images and suggestions – from my own experience.

I was about eight years old when something really cool and funny happened to me at my parents' home. My parents had an open-plan kitchen. Dividing the kitchen from the dining room was a 3 feet wall with a nice mahogany top acting as a stand where my mum had usually two rattan baskets. The one on the left had always fruit inside and the other had usually bread. That was just the way it was. There was fruit in one and bread in the other. When I was about ten, I got hungry in the evening and decided to go to the kitchen to prepare myself a nice crusty roll with butter and strawberry jam. I went in the kitchen and switched on the light, went to one the cabinets and took the jam out and then into the fridge and got the butter and took a knife from one of the drawers. I was all set up and the only thing I was missing now was the roll. So I remember well looking at the roll inside the basket and after I picked up the one that looked tastier. I then followed by stretching my arm towards the basket and opened my hand and grabbed a roll but instantly as I touched the bread I jumped back in fear. What the hell! I thought at the time. Without even looking I knew I had not picked up bread. My hand told me that. The shape and texture did not match. Then I shook my head and blinked my eyes a few times and there they were. Lemons! Lemons! It was summertime, and my parents' lemon tree was bending over with so much weight. My mum had decided to pick a few and for no reason in particular she had changed my world. The fact is that my brain got used to the image of rolls inside that basket and my eyes saw what I wanted to see. But that wasn't the case on that day. Both my eyes and my brain saw the same image: grey, a newly invented shade of grey. If that had been the end of the story, maybe I would just believe that I needed to sleep more or maybe read less or see less movies too. The fact is that if you recall I mentioned that a strange and small object had been dropped from above the Death Line. And it was a small object, in fact, but what matters here is that it was, in fact, an object dropping down slowly hanging to what looked like one of those sky-blue weather balloons. My eyes fixed on it like in a trance. At that moment I crossed to the other side of the A259 and went down towards the beach. Running would have to wait because this was too transcendent for me. As I went closer to the beach the weather changed dramatically from sunny to cloudy and windy, and everyone abandoned the area. It felt as if I was immune to that or maybe I was just hypnotised in such a manner that the surroundings could not affect me.

My eyes fixed on that object as it slowly approached the beach crossing wind and clouds and rain gently as if on a beautiful sunny day. I was in disbelief, but I couldn't stop my body from going to the beach exactly where I usually sit to relax. I sat down in peace. The balloon looked as if it was coming in my direction and it was. It took probably an hour until it gently landed on my legs. Wind and rain had been hitting like waves against rocks and yet I didn't feel anything. I was alone there at that moment and it felt that I was on my own in the entire planet. On my lap was now a wooden heart-shaped photo frame without any picture in it but engraved at the back there was the picture on the immaculate heart of Mary. The sky cleared in a few seconds and the wind stopped and the sun hit gently on my face warming up my body. I was at peace, but I couldn't at that moment understand the meaning of what had just happened in there. I felt in my heart that I had seen that picture before, but where? And why was that heart engraved on the back of that simple and humble wooden frame? I knew why but I could not see it then. When people lose faith and stop believing they start missing the signs, start looking at things that are there but they cannot see them. Later on, everything will make sense, and I will see clearly the face in that photo frame, but for now there's nothing in there. I grabbed that frame, looked at it as if a miracle had just happened and decided to go home instead of going running. The planes kept flying lower as never seen. I don't remember getting home. My friend Don't Matter was still there. He was sitting down quiet at the kitchen table having his meal, some sort of improvised chicken Chow Mein. Too quiet, I would say. It felt as if he was entranced by something coming from his phone. He was watching a video on YouTube. He never saw me or heard me, so I took the chance to go to my room and put the wooden photo frame in my room and change into more comfortable clothes. I followed by going back to the kitchen where he was still in the position and same spirits. To be honest, my mind was too troubled with the recent event, but I tried to keep it together and asked him if everything was all right. He gave a crazy disbelief look and asked me if I had seen the news. That was obviously a rhetorical question because I stopped watching news many years ago. When you lose trust in information the best thing to do is to stop wasting your energy with disinformation, right? If we think that probably whoever controls banks, controls also the economy and therefore TV, what's the point of giving them attention? This might be a too dramatic approach to reality but it's mine, and I'm happy with that. So when he asked that I naturally said no, I haven't.

'Really, you haven't seen this?' And he balanced his phone on the table so that he could share more disinformation (I mean the news he was watching) broadcasting on BBC news. You know when kids do something wrong like breaking their parents' favourite jar or the neighbours' window and they find the craziest, stupid and nonsense excuses not to explain how it happened, or that it was an accident but just put the blame on someone else or allege that they haven't even noticed it or whatever? Well, that was the sort of nonsense BBC was broadcasting. I believe that the human brain is drawn to whatever caught his attention and that will vary on the individual interests of the subject. In my case I have faith that my brain turns its attention mainly for real and interesting matters even though I like fast cars and fast food (rarely) or watching football. But when it comes to news or even documentaries my brain has a very powerful crap codifier. In a way my mind was still aborted with the recent event and when you have journalist, world leaders and scientist and pope and priest and common people (humans) talking and showing off on TV about the motives why aeroplanes had now to travel under the 15,000 feet line (Death Line) and magnetic fields, atmospheric layers and signs of the apocalypse and how the balance of life on Earth would change forever; even with what had just happened to me something wasn't sticking in my brain. Bollocks, like they say around here. Don't Matter was overwhelmed. He had a disbelief expression in his eyes when that moment a few planes passed by roaring very low. The sound caught our attention and gave me a crazy look asking at the same time what I thought about all that. I really didn't know what I thought of that but I learned not to panic about the unknown, and with that I said that I had no idea but I was sure that someone would very soon give an explanation about all that and that everything would be fine. I felt that I had not given him the answer he wanted but deep in my mind that was how I felt about it. Everything is going to be fine. We live in an ever-changing world, and that's the truth. Every now and then inexplicable phenomena occur but, man, science and time explain and take care of everything. Time is the best counsellor and best healer of this amazing cosmos we live in. I felt at that point the need of telling him or someone else what happened to me before but I once learned that every so often the best thing to do with what we know is to keep it under the hat. It was a fact that with the recent developments on Earth maybe if a perfect Jon Doe like me went and told a story like the one that happened earlier, maybe some would believe it but probably the great majority wouldn't even give me attention. As I mentioned before our brain turns its attention to what is more significant within the realm of our upbringing. And in the end, it was a smart call not to tell anyone about it because later every Tom, Dick, and Harry that went on live feed to testify about similar events would mysteriously disappear. What was about to happen could only be understood by true believers. Only people of conviction could see past the mist. The pillar of faith is belief, and its body is miracle. Science was about to go back to the Dark Ages.

CHAPTER 3

News from another dimension

In Heaven and Hell; March the 9th 1999.

Tomorrow is big day, my husband. You need to stop playing those games and start thinking about the end of the
world. It will happen in less than a year. Are you listening
to me? God damn it! God, can you stop that shit and do
something useful for once in your eternity? It was Mary.
She looked like an infuriated dragon spitting fire through
her mouth. And she carried on like a proper housewife
picking on a useless husband. Just because you know
everything it doesn't mean that you don't have to prepare
for tomorrow! You will not embarrass me again in front of
everyone (all saints and angels and the Devil and his

demons) like you did nearly 2,000 years ago! I have had enough of looking crazy and crying in vein. But God did not turn around from his white chair yet. He was playing Lara Croft in his experimental version of Xbox one. Let's say he had very good connections inside Microsoft and he had a special deal with Boyd Multerer. He managed to try the console more than 15 years before it went to the market. Mary started now crying like on the day she saw Christ losing the brightness in his eyes and before he was resurrected. She went to the huge balcony in their immense room that faced north over what seemed a recreation of the savannahs of Africa. God dearly loved very much his creations and more than the universe with all the stars and the planets he preferred the animals. One can say that because he is all seeing he didn't have the need to have that amazing landscape from his bedroom, but then again he could as only he could wish, and on the other hand just because we know something or someone that doesn't mean that we don't have to show or tell that person that we love them. They need to know, right? God was a bit annoyed with Mary's act but did not show it. As normal he kept a serene look and started by telling Mary that she was too nervous and without a reason. Everything would be fine with tomorrow's summit and that she needed to chill out a bit. She pretended not to listen to him and kept crying – less – but in a lower tone. She had her attention, but she had not yet listened to what she wanted; something like: I'm sorry. You are right. I was distracted with the game and the matters of the world at the same time and didn't notice you. I'm sorry, my sweetheart. Please forgive me. But God was in the end a man and we know how many of us usually do exactly the opposite of what we should when it comes to interacting with other humans, but especially with women. God walked gently and soundlessly to the balcony and stopped beside Mary. They both stared in silence for a while at the savannah in front. All sorts of tropical colours and animal shapes on the ground and in the skies could be seen in the distance. God increased slightly the echo coming from the distance because he knew he felt calmer with that. Mary did not say anything immediately but tilted her head to the left where God was and gave him a disapproving smile like what parents give to children when they do something wrong but they still tell them that they loved them with that expression. God decided to make things right and asked Mary about Jesus. Your son, is he still in bed? Even in eternity God decided that having timed days would some-how balance his Heaven. You know what I mean. Rules are the basis of human society and they were the basis of

Heaven ever since God decided to create one. If it had not been for the natural soundtrack of Africa playing from the distance, I think Mary would lose it again and would break the porcelain again, so she kept it together. Nevertheless, she opened her heart and told God what she thought about what he had just said. She did it in a very diplomatic way. My son, what do you mean? Our son, you meant, for sure. Our son is still sleeping, as you very well know, poor child. You know how he spends his days listening to prayers and how all that makes him tired and confused. He doesn't have an easy life like many around here. She went silent. God went silent for a while too. God felt that she was right but did not tell her; instead he snapped his fingers and changed the landscape that seemed to be a place somewhere in the Caribbean islands and said: 'You love this place, don't you?'

Mary knew why he did this and she knew him too well to try to change him, so she nodded yes with her head and just kept quiet watching the yellow sand, the clear waters and the coconut trees framing the picture. God followed by telling her that she could go there any time she wanted. She couldn't take it anymore and exploded. Her expression and her tone altered dramatically, and she screamed at him and abandoned the room, saying this on her way out: 'You know what? I have had enough of this bullshit and I have had enough of you! You don't want to think about tomorrow as usual, it's your problem! But I'll tell you something: you had better create me an end of the world very soon or you won't lay your hands on me for the next thousands…' and she made a pause – 'millennium!' – She fired like a bazooka! 'And I'm not joking!' Another missile fired. 'And your breakfast and your lunch today you can take care of that yourself! Why don't just snap your fingers and make it happen! I'm sure it's easy for you!' And she left the room infuriated.

God exhaled deeply and snapped the landscape back to Africa and thought: I damn myself. Why did I create women? But she is right, as always. I need to do something about the year 2000. But how can I tell her that I will not end the world on Eearth? He looked at the blue sky above and he smiled. He had an idea. And let's be honest here, if God can't sell his idea, who will? It's very cool to be God. Being God is much different from being a Jesus. You don't have to explain anything because in the end no one really knows who you are. God is but a conceptual ideal. On the other hand, Jesus had a body, a life and his philosophies, maybe not quite the same as his apostles preached after and definitely very different from those of the new church but still a new humanistic reality. Even if most of that was inspired in early oral stories and myths spread around the world's civilisation, that cannot diminish his merit because for every new idea there has to be an historical background supporting it. Evolution doesn't happen by snapping fingers. Evolution is an everlasting process moving somewhere far away from reasoning. We can imagine how things will but – for now – we can't travel in time. Recent developments in that area have proved that travelling in time is not scientifically possible, but then again in a world of Gods and beliefs what is science and knowledge? Science is maybe just another form of pre-potency?

God was bored. He thought of his preferred white sheep chair and the chair appeared behind him. He sat down watching Africa on his 100K projection known as GODMAX. It was about 9am now. He was waiting for Mary and his breakfast. Mary had a very special heart indeed. She was a bit bad tempered in the morning. Well, like many women, and I wonder why. But in the end, she loved her husband and very soon she would appear with an angel bringing God an international breakfast. If that did not happen, God would just make it happen anyway and that was how tedious his life was. Gods are like people in the end.

You are unhappy when you are poor because we wish for something more and then when we have everything, we wish to have even more or too have the apparent simple life of shepherds.   It is very right the saying that we cannot please both Greeks and Trojans. God tilted his head towards Mary and the eunuch and gave them a smile. The angel smiled back. Mary tilted her head the other way and thought: I hope you don't choke with it. And God listened to her thought and spoke with her directly into her soul. Oh, common sweetheart; that isn't a very Christian thing to say, is it? And you know I know what irony and sarcasm are – I invented it? Remember? Plagues, floods, diseases and wars? But it's OK. I know why you are the way you are. But please don't worry, my love; everything is going to be just fine. And he smiled into her soul; he gave her attention and understanding. What else do all of us want in the end if not that? God went back to his game. He thought about talking to a few of his saints and angels about the next day's summit, but there was still time. He would do it after lunch or so. For now, it was time to test the game and the new console. But his peace was about to end. Hey buddy, how are you doing? It was the Devil talking inside his head. What are up to, my friend? Let me guess; are you playing games again? Ahaha! Ahaha! God tilted his head a few times in disapproval but didn't answer. You don't talk to me anymore? The Devil carried on bugging God's peace. Do you know where I am sticking my fingers and cock? Do you want to make a guess? Inside three virgins! Well, they are not that virgin anymore! Ahaha! Ahaha! Come on, cocksucker, talk to me GOOOD, damn you! Ahaha! Ahaha! God was getting upset now. He missed a shot at an enemy inside a tomb and God is perfect. Come on, buddy, talk to me! And the Devil followed by singing Charlie Puth's song: 'We don't talk anymore…' And he carried on singing and laughing and telling God that he could carry on doing that for all eternity. God couldn't take it anymore and went: Fuck you and fuck your house, you devil damn fallen bastard. What the fuck do you want now? God ended up creating an earthquake in Asia due to this moment. Well, things happen for a reason, so they say. Ahaha! Ahaha! Come on, buddy, calm down. What's going on? Did you miss a shot in your game, did you? Ahaha! God interfered. Can you cut the crap and just go straight to the point? I have a lot of things to do and worry about today. Uh, you are such a busy guy, are you not? – Ahaha. The Devil loved these moments with God. In his room the Almighty kept tilting his head and praying for the help of his son just for some help in that instant. Hey, listen, my friend, let the boy sleep, OK? I'm sure he has been very busy lately doing your job. Ahaha! It was too much. God had to try to put the Devil in his place. Hey, listen: you like your virgins, right? You should know that I'm very well aware of your deal with Saint Peter about trading the little girls for hydro honey, OK? So please go straight to the point or I'll hand the keys to Father Cruz. The Devil gave one more controlled laugh and asked God to chill out. No need for that, mate. Listen, it's about tomorrow's meeting. What time do you want me there? Ahaha! Ahaha. The Devil was a happy fellow, never losing a chance for a good giggle. God took a moment to think about it for the first time and then he told the Devil. Well, I'm thinking that Mary could prepare lunch for all of us, so we don't need to wake up too early. I'm thinking about 11am. Then we can have lunch and I'm thinking of maybe carrying on the meeting until teatime and by then everything should be sorted. Is that OK? Oh, and you and demons have to use aluminium hats. And the Devil made a short moment of silence. OK, it's fine with me, but did you say eleven or 'aleven'? Ahaha! Ahaha! Whatever! I know what's going to happen and I'm OK with the decision. So, tomorrow at 'aaleven' I'll be there with my demons. Talk later, cocksucker! Ahaha! Ahaha. God exhaled deeply and thought: Fucking hell! He thought: fi-

nally, a moment of silence. I can still hear you, coooock-
sucker! Ahaha! Ahaha! And the Devil carried on playing
with his Commodore 64. God couldn't take any more shit;
he quickly put his aluminium hat on his head; the only real
protection in Heaven against mind reading. Ah, finally,
bastard.

God ended up being brought down to reality by the
Devil. In a way everything has a balance and one cannot be
without the other. For every night we will have a new day
and all the opposites you can think of. Surely, we couldn't
dream of a good God without the existence of an evil God
called the Devil. About the second one many things have
been said but he was never accused of plagues or apocalypses and other good and very Christian things like the inquisition paedophilia. Sometimes I wonder who is good or
bad in this history but that will be a subject of another
story. This story is called Oliwia. And I remember well the
beauty and the peacefulness of her image. Someone like her
can only be part of this crazy drama because I believe
there's yet another stage of perfection that neither Men,
Women nor Gods have up till now created the right conceptual word to express it. Maybe one day I'll invent that new
word myself. Now, going back to Heaven, God decided it
was finally time to do something about the summit for the

next day. With that in mind he went to his balcony again and sat down on his chair and started informing his workers. He started by informing his angels and his saints. The message was simple, and if we were in Brighton during summer time the main idea was something like this: according to the BBC weather forecast, tomorrow the sun will shine again and I'm inviting you all to join me by the pier, after 6 pm, for a BBQ followed by a bonfire. No need to worry about food or drinks because I'm taking care of everything this time. The major difference is that this 'summit' would take place in the savannahs of Africa and Mary would take care of everything as per usual. God knew she would not let him down and that she was very keen for detail in days like those. And that was it; message delivered. Another day, another dollar, thought God, and he went back to Lara Croft. In one of the other rooms Jesus was still sleeping with his aluminium hat on his head. I often wonder how Woody Allen knew that was the way of things in Heaven. Well, one cannot say the man was short of imagination, so I guess that was why he discerned the effectiveness of foil. Jesus? Jesus? Are you OK, my son? Jesus? It's nearly 11, my son, you need to wake up. There are millions of prayers and requests jamming the wireless connections in Heaven.

'Son? Please wake up. You know how your father gets upset when he can't telepath information or play his games streaming from Earth, don't you? Please, my son, wake up.' Jesus, you know how he blew up that stair one year ago... and Mary carried on trying to wake up Jesus like my mum used to do with me during the cold winters so I could go to school. – Really? Na. Don't think so. I have a headache. – That's how I felt when my mother tried to take out of my bed; that cosy place so similar to being a baby living in amniotic bath; happy like a fish in a tank. Jesus couldn't listen to her. That's how powerful his aluminium hat was. Mary knew what to do but she was afraid of his re-action. Not long ago he had slapped her on her face when she woke him up leaving a visible mark on her for about ten years. That's what you get for disturbing 'the one' dur-ing his Christian deserved rest. Let the man sleep, I would say. Let him dream of a better world. She had to go for it, however. She stretched her arm from the distance and cuffed his hair gently and said: 'Please, my son, wake up.' Jesus trembled a bit like when our body has sudden changes of temperature. He was still sleeping but he was already sighing something like: 'What? What? No! No! Yes. Yes. Maybe – oh, in my father's name, no, no, no, no...' and he jumped out of bed like a maniac. What the

Heaven! Where am I? What's going on here? What? Yes!
No!'

Poor semi-god; it may not be hard to create a new
religion, but it's a different business to keep it, especially
when everyone else on Earth cared more about the profit
that could be made out of it rather than live by his example.
God has no doubt a twisted sense of humour. Knowing
what was coming for the next centuries, why wouldn't he
just give his son eternal life like vampires have and keep
the boy on Earth taking care of the operations? Well, I
guess he was too busy playing other kinds of games. At the
time, all those years ago, he was probably busy playing
Arkanoid on his ZX Spectrum 128KGOD. How else could
Sinclair Research think of 8-bit? Jesus! Oh Jesus! Please,
oh Jesus! Jesus. Mary knew how to calm down her son with
that suggestion. Mary entranced Jesus back to his faith. Jesus was online, but because he had his hat on, he was only
on one frequency; the frequency of the moment that we see.
Hi Mother. How are you feeling today? Is he already up?
Did he have his breakfast seeing Africa? Was he Himself?
And Jesus looked gently and calmly to his mother knowing
that his love would make her forget God's world. And so
she did. Sometimes what better than just close your eyes
for a few seconds and breathe deeply and just let go from a

top of a mountain like a wing, just a wing taken by the wind flying over no sin. Mary and the true believers could do that: fly. That and cry a lot just like a good actor. Oh, this and that and there you go; tears falling rain. Mary put a smile on her face and told him: that's why I love you so much! You are so clever! Oh myself! It was not because of God, your father – egocentric bastard! Doesn't even know who his father was! Mary took the chance to have these thoughts because both God and Jesus were wearing the foil hats and she was lucky with the Devil too because he was exhausting his too. And when I say exhausting his too I mean it almost literally; nothing like a relaxed blowjob without any interference in the waves of pleasure , – OOH my God, would the Devil say with a naughty smile on his face every time he had one. And Mary carried on: well, at least you have inherited something good from your father, Mary declared, looking at her son's window. On the window there was a live scene of the Mount of Olives. Jesus tilted his head right and left with a smile on his face. So you didn't forget about tomorrow? She asked. How could I, my dear mother? Answered Jesus while serving himself a mint tea and biting a bit of chapatti bread – very cheap to keep, that boy. Good sighted her. Good? What doesn't that mean, Mother? Questioned the chosen one? (Don't forget about the hat). Well, you know why...the time has come, my son...finally...all those that plotted and preached against you and your commandments will be brought to justice. I don't want to seem awful with what I'm about to say but I 'kind of saw' an evil smile on Mary's face; you know, like the smile of every evil queen from a fairy tale story like the 'sleeping beauty', for example. There was definitely something twisted with her expression; a touch of oil in a huge canvas looking like trauma; like a mix of conscious, subconscious and unconscious instinctive brushes of red desire for a greyish justice; her justice; Mary the ultimate Supreme Court; very weird... if you ask me, especially coming from the wife of God and the mother of Jesus. I guess that maybe we are all humans in the completion. Jesus took his hat. He wanted to know what really was going on inside his mother's head but let's not forget the importance of parents in this story... let's remember that I'm dedicating this story to my father and that he knew me better than anyone else – the school you are attending now? I've been there already! – He told me this so many times. Mary abandoned the room just after her son removed his hat and told him that he knew what had to be done and that she loved him very much and that she wished he had a very pleasant day inputting and outputting zeros and ones coming and going from Earth. The only words Jesus got from her mind that made any sense were: for your father's imaginary wisdom just make it happen! Even I'm tired of this shit – it's just too many numbers…and these were the last thoughts Jesus read from her mind: 01000110 01101001 01101110 01100001 01101100 01101100 01111001 00100000 01110100 01101000 01100101 00100000 01100101 01101110 01100100 00100000 01101001 01110011 00100000 01101110 01100101 01100001 01110010. He nodded his head in disapproval and went back in his memory to the time he sat upon the Mount of Olives when his disciples came to him privately, asking him about the future and about the signs that would alert the believers of the end of the world.   – Did I express myself the wrong way in that night? Or did they misunderstand what I was saying? Maybe there was too much wine involved. Oh, Mother, I'm afraid you will be very disappointed tomorrow. I know what my father is plotting and even though I don't agree with his plan at least there will be no end of the world so soon. I never wanted anything like that for mankind. What I wished then and now is just for them to find their own peace of mind and whatever makes them truly happy. – That's my boy. – interfered God. Crap after crap. – added the Devil. Jesus put his hat on again and thought about love. In the end not many people understood truly what he preached and why he willingly went to the cross. I have a theory; when someone had so much love in his mind, as he did, he could see beyond the stars because he was in fact part of the universe and when you understand that, nothing, not even the idea of death frightens you because you know the universe has something special waiting for you – but that's just my theory.

On Earth chaos was giving place to balance. People couldn't understand the new regulations; the Death Line, the explanations about that and mostly could not comprehend their role in life. I was still troubled with what had happened to me. Somehow I knew that a miracle had just happened and that I was an important piece of that miracle, but I wasn't yet quite sure if I had been the one provoking that wonder or if I was just another random and inexplicable event of the cosmos. That's how people feel when they think they have beliefs but allow doubts to cloud your reasoning. That's how I was feeling in that moment on Earth. And there's no shame in saying it: I felt lost. This story will go back to Earth very soon, but for now we need to go back to Heaven so everything makes sense in the end. The big day had come. God sent an invitation with the time and place for everyone using his own frequency; GAM and it was no surprise for all of them that the summit would take place in his gardens of Africa at eleven am (aleven am said in Scottish). Mary and her ladies took care of the food and the beverage and Joseph and the Pope Pius IX took care of making the tables and chairs for everyone. There would be only 16 saints, 9 angels and 8 demons attending this summit joining God, Mary and Jesus and the Devil. It was an easy job for the pair of the Josephs. God was very proud of them when he saw their work. It was a sight, that huge round table sliced of the biggest giant sequoia tree from California – and no need to stress about it, my green friends, because this cut came out of God's private collection. Oh, in His name, and the chairs? Perfection! Very close to authentic Manga Chairs by Nendo. Beautiful simple and eccentric just like sushi. Those chairs would somehow inspire the chair of one Throne of medieval Game, or the other way around. That's how intricate reality and the transcendent are for me. They were made of sequoia and not metal – calm down, greens because even in Heaven there's respect for trees and even the leaves were fed to the animals of Africa and the branches were put in the deserts on Earth to give it a less inhospitable look.

In a blink the moment came, and everyone was in Africa for the big day. God sat down on a huge rock waiting for the whispering to stop. Like on Earth they gathered in groups and bitched about everything. About the way they were dressed. About whom they were. You know groupies, right? Our neighbour's house, car and wife are always better than ours. Vanity and emptiness are unfortunately some of the motors of society. God was waiting patiently. He has all the time in the universe because he is the space also. At last everyone was quiet. Demons, saints and angels were wearing Byzantine dresses in shades of red for the demons, green and blue for the angels. The demons had rich golden jewellery like rap stars. The saints had one single pendant each and the angels had no accessories. Mary had a long and modest pearl dress with a Vermeer blue veil and a pendant with her heart. Jesus had a seamless woven robe covering all his body and a small wooden cross in his hand that Joseph had carved earlier in the morning from the giant sequoia. All of them were wearing sandals. The Devil is the Devil and God is God, right. So what do you think both of them were wearing? The Devil couldn't hide a naughty smile from his face. Of course, he couldn't. For once in his life he has surpassed God. He had a neon red Stuart Hughes Diamond Edition suit and with a grey shirt underneath and a pair of the finest alligator skin shoes by Amedeo Testoni. He was so proud of himself: he had no jewellery. He brought as the only accessory a five feet tall mirror and that was it. God couldn't hide his envy, but he didn't emit any thought about it. He would never give that pleasure to The Devil. About God, well, he wasn't as shiny as his arch-rival, but he was still very fashionable and let's not forget they were all in Africa. So, God had an Amosu Vanquish II Bespoke suit and…? Do you want to try to guess what sort of shoes he had? White All Star. They took their time and kept their distance but at 'aleven' all of them stood straight and tall around the big rock God placed near the huge round table. The monkeys would finish setting up the table with food and drinks and elephants would finish creating a nice shade over the table with branches also from the se-quoia. The time had come. God started to thank the chosen ones for coming. 'I would like to thank you, my good old friends, for being here today' (and with this he put a smile on the Devil's and demons' faces). I must say they all looked very well with their aluminium   hats on.

CHAPTER 4

News from Heaven

Meanwhile, on Earth, things were not looking that good. I kept thinking exactly the same; I had told my friend Don't Matter. Everything is going to be fine. I decide not to hide the wooden frame I had apparently received from the skies. I placed it by my bedside where I could look at it every moment. It would take me a while to know what it intended. What was the sublime meaning of that artefact? Where had I seen it earlier? I knew I had seen it before, but I couldn't remember where. Whoever had sent that piece of wood had a plan for me. I was sure about it. But who sent it, and why? I felt compelled to think about it every day. I would wake up in the morning and look at it; I would write about it and have it in mind all the time and even my drawings or paintings would show unconscious messages from it. I felt deeply entranced by it. I searched the web numerous times trying to put a face to that frame, but I never really found one like that and the few that had pictures in it didn't make any sense at all. You know when we have the feeling that something doesn't belong there like when we try to find the differences of two similar drawings in a newspaper and sooner or later we fix our eyes and our brain ends up showing us what doesn't belong; the dissimilarity? Well, that frame was different but consistent at the same time. That frame fitted somewhere important; I just didn't know where. By hook or by crook it was clear to me that only focusing my mind on it and thinking about it I could unveil a clear message. The world was falling apart. Most people knew that there was more to it than an issue with the magnetic field of our planet. Everyone knows that we live under a permanent web of lies woven by not much more than a dozen tarantulas. There's a plan for all of us, but we are kept ignorant about it until the day there are no more resources to create profit. When that day comes, God helps us because we will turn into expendable numbers. Well, in reality that's what the tarantulas think because the truth is that when the people unite the scenario changes. A very good example of that is love. Unfortunately, bad people allied with time can make people forget how invincible the power of love is. When I think about our actual Christian

Church, I feel ashamed to have been baptised Christian but if I travel back about 2,010 years ago things change dramatically. If we think about Jesus and his message when understanding how a voice preaching a renewed faith based on love and respect was and still is able to unite people; millions united by a single voice that loved and believed in love. It's a simple thought; if you have love in your heart, you will not have hate; in the same way if you want peace, you will not create wars. Sadly, for the general population what really matters for those few spiders is not what they preach, and the best proof of that is that when you think that you know what is better for other people you already forgot the concept of freedom. How can one be free if you cannot create your own universe? Maybe if we were not kept caged by the rules of society, maybe we could all be gods. But this story has no pretension of a philosophical essay, so I'll stop theorising about it because many books have been written about it and I'm sure that in one of them there will be a theory coherent with everyone's ideals, including mine. I do not want to say that they are all right; correct and incorrect are very ephemeral concepts; let's not forget what darkness the Polish Copernicus brought to the enlightened times of the Christian Church. Let's say the man was so wrong that Christians had to create the Inquisition to prove he was wrong about his observations of sky seen from the Earth. Of course, he was wrong about the heliocentric theory and the proof of that is that his student Galileo admitted all his theories were wrong (I'm being ironic for those that don't know much about history? If you don't know what I'm talking about, there's a very simple solution to understand that; just Google: geocentric, heliocentric and inquisition and you will understand what I'm saying). I need to say that things like that and hundreds of other similar displays of ignorance might have been the seeds of my disbeliefs. Luckily for me and for all intelligent human beings the ability of reasoning ideas and concepts allows us to see beyond that. Most things about faith and religion are bullshit; it's a fact, but not everything is fezzes. There's hope in past praying. There are lessons to be taken from it all. The secret is very simple. I can't talk for other people because I'm not a tarantula, but I can talk about the things I've learned in my life. With this mind I remember my literature classes and the teachings of my best educators: the only way we can learn is by listening or reading and interpreting and comprehending the underlying meaning of any message. Ignorance is for me an addiction or a misunderstanding, but that's just my opinion. Everyone is different.

Everyone has different dreams, right? But there's nothing wrong in sharing the same dreams, is there?

Planes kept vanishing in smoke. Men are in the end big children. What do usually boys do when they are told they can't do something? They do exactly the opposite. It's in the human nature to dare or die. How many planes would have to disappear in smoke until pilots finally understood that the Death Line was real? Whatever was happening was kept a secret, but an urgent solution was needed; another lie. I wasn't worried about it, honestly. Don't ask me why? In my mind there was only one, though. Everything will be fine. But how could I and that frame belong in some sort of higher plan that would maybe help what had happened? I'm just a simple man and my beliefs are yet a sketch of an unknown painting. No matter what doubts I had in my mind in those days, something was about to change. TVs worldwide started broadcasting news of a G10 summit. The leaders of the free world were meeting in a secret location to sort out this enigma. Obviously being the creator of this story, their secrecy doesn't work with me, so I will tell you all about it. You need to know what's going on. It's only fair that mankind can finally understand what the Heaven and Hell is going on. Bear in mind that impossible is nothing. Accept what I am about to tell you as something normal and something that can happen when you have either a lot of faith or even more imagination and that there's nothing wrong in choosing to be a simple sheep. Freedom is just that. Choosing whatever makes us complete. What we need to remember is that for every decision and act we make or do there's a repercussion or effect. Call it karma; call it fame or call it death or jail, but something will definitely happen when we stop conforming to what we were told was the right thing. The dead-on thing is up to us to discover. So, in the sequence of this strange event on Earth and in the eminence of the raising up of anarchic ideas of people that could unbalance the wellbeing and prosperity of a few and the great design of others, the following email was sent by God to ten of the most brilliant humans on this planet a week before the TVs started broadcasting news about a secret and necessary summit between the chosen ones:

From: God

To: António Guterres, Jean-Claude Juncker, Donald Trump, Vladimir Putin, Theresa May, Angela Merkel, Emmanuel Macron, Justin Trudeau, Sergio Mattarella and Shinzō Abe (the pagan lover being left for last, of course)

Subject: Death Line.

My fellow followers, true believers of my faith and the finest example of what I have ever designed in this infant universe in which as was lucky to be the first to reason. I know that you are well and that getting worried with this anomaly in your planet, and that's the reason why I decided to contact you and give you a hand to sort out this messy situation (even God finds it hard to admit mistakes and say I'm sorry; it was my fault. It's never easy to admit an error, is it, especially when your name is God. For him this was no longer a mistake but an opportunity for mankind to find his way out of darkness again; nothing like a good equation to evolve the grey mass called brain). I know that you need to offer a solution to your sheep there on Earth. I'm aware of the chaos rising up in your society and I know the reason why all that is happening there. Well, I need to tell you that this is the work of the Devil. That ingrate bastard betrayed my trust again. I'll explain you everything and I will need your help to fix this, OK? (God and his inverted psychology). As you must have noticed the subject of this email is the Death Line. I came up with this name because this is the name already inputted in many minds there on Earth and the morale of your people is already so down and I don't want to create any more disappointments. The Death Line is the name of this phenomenon and you know well by now what happens to those who try to cross the line: 'In the sweat of thy face shalt thou eat bread, till thou return unto ground; for out of it wast thou taken: for dust thou art, and unto dust shalt thou return.'– Genesis 3:19 (King James Version). This needs to end, my dear friends. You need to control your people better, that's why I chose you to take care of the operations there on Earth. I'll leave that to you too; how to control their minds. I have too many beings to take care of in the immense universe, as I'm sure you can imagine. Well, I'm actually in a bit of a hurry, so I'll go straight to the point. My dear gentlemen and friends, about 18 years of your time ago my good friend Saint Peter came to me, a few weeks after an important summit took place here in Heaven, with a slight concern regarding the vacancies for souls here in Heaven. It looks as if you have been doing a very good job there on Earth. Naturally, because I'm the creator of all things, I listened to his apprehensions, but to be fair, I did not give it much attention at the time because I was busy testing one of the future models for Xbox and you know well how that is something of utmost priority for me; even I don't remember when I first started playing games in this universe. Well, but it is not important now. What you need to know is that just before the spring of 1999 I organised a summit in my savannahs of Africa and invited a few of my best counsellors to talk about the end of your world. As you can see by now that hasn't happened yet – and there is no need to thank me – but the reason that hasn't occurred yet is because I came up with a brilliant idea of not having to reset your world through a final judgment day; instead I thought of keeping the souls of dead bodies in one of the several layers of your atmosphere just until we managed to sort out some more vacancies here in Heaven and until I or my son Jesus could separate the sheep and hopefully send a few to Hell as it's becoming a very empty place thanks to me. But unfortunately, my son Jesus got a bit lazy and is waking up too late and has too many humans thinking he is Aladdin. And I, as you well know, apart from my games, have innumerable other things to worry about. Well, all this said, during that summit things were decided that are affecting your planet now. The Devil was the one choosing in what layer to put the souls waiting for judgment. I learned later that the combination of the chemicals of the stratosphere with the ones of the soul can provoke a very deadly reaction. Unfortunately, until this problem is solved you will not be able to travel higher than half-way to the troposphere as from that point on it becomes highly unstable. The reason why you cannot see what's going on above the Death Line is because I've painted your skies with a lovely camouflage picture of the firmaments above and for that you can thank Leonardo and Raphael. And they did such a great job, did they not? I love their work, don't you? I know how all this must look hard to understand and believe but I know you trust what I'm telling you as the truth, and again I also know that you discern that everything was done to allow you to carry on doing your great design there on Earth and what a great job you are doing down there, my friends. I need to tell you once again how proud I am of your work, worthy, no doubt, of a seat on my table when your day comes. Well, I hope you understood what I have just told you and how urgent it is for all of you to get together and put your brilliant minds thinking of ways of fixing this matter. It's in your best interest to find a solution. I will now carry on playing my Lara Croft – amazing version this one – and please rest assured that I'm also thinking of ways of sorting all this mess out. You can count on me always for any queries and thank me and damn the Devil for what he has done to you all. OK, now I need to go back to my experimental Xbox Ten version and play my Lara Croft – it will be amazing, I can assure you that God blinked an eye and the message went instantly to everyone's inbox. Messages from God for the chosen ones work like hypnotic suggestions. Once you get one your brain shifts to them no matter what you are doing. In the exact same moment, all the ten guardians of the Earth knew it and rushed to their computer checking it. Apart from the Japanese Prime Minister all of them felt some joy and hope knowing that God had not forgotten them in this troubled moment on the planet. Shinzō Abe was playing Dragon Ball GT and having a miso soup at the same time. He felt the incoming message and immediately put his aluminium hat on his head before thinking; what does this selfish double-faced bastard want from us this time? More lies, I trust, and he carried on playing his game and having his soup until curiosity made him check his email in the end. The other magnificent nine were caught up in the most different situations and it's not important to mention them all because very soon they will be together and will have the opportunity to once again show their feelings about this email. Maybe it's worth mentioning that Donald Trump was still in bed building a great wall made out of Legos, his version of the Great Wall of China. The only difference was that his would be called The Great Trump Wall and the invaders were no warriors but mainly gardeners and fruit pickers coming from Mexico. Merkel was in her room dressed up with a tight rubber suit sodomising a black man and telling him to tell her what she loves the most hearing: You are the master! – Who is the master? – You are the master! – What do I love the most? – Interest! – And who are you? – I'm no one! Everyone has their crazy stuff, right? António Guterres was lying down in a beach in the Algarve having sardines and drinking red wine thinking about ways of uniting all the sardines in the world in a big pool so he could be the sardine master. Theresa May was in the loo thinking of ways to convince her people that her Brexit ideas were actually good for the future of England; and how right she was. The monetary value of her coin had dropped nearly 30% in the last year. Come on, that's good isn't it? Unstable markets; it's brilliant! As for the rest of the other members of the G10, they were doing even more interesting things but not worth mentioning now. The most important summit in the history of mankind was about to take place. I was in the living room writing a tragic romance called *Morse* about the impossible love between two persons of different cultures and different countries. A true love that would have a tragic ending – Romeo and Juliet style but with a twist in the end, but that's another novel for another reading. As I was saying, I was there alone in the living room trying to concentrate my mind for creation. I usually choose Japanese music to inspire myself because of the dissimilar rhythm it has from most common music on this planet. Japanese music is better for my creative process because I don't see writing as a mathematical equation under the rules of rhythm. Writing is more related to the beat of my heart and that pace varies with my mood, and it involves thinking and breathing processes that one can no doubt relate to music, but it is still very unlike me. Like I said before: everyone has his own crazy stuff inside their soul. I'm no different from anyone else except maybe the fact that I usually am a positive person and have faith in myself. Like I was saying, I was there in my living room looking at the ceiling trying to find the right words to express my thoughts when my troubled friend Don't Matter rushed in showing me another video from You Tube, again, news from BBC One. This time it was about a secret gathering of the G10. I think that was the first day that officially the concept of Death Line was mentioned. There are spies everywhere and you are probably thinking that WikiLeaks must be involved in this, but I believe that for most occasions information is deliberately put out in the streets by those who have a secret and future agenda. I'll explain; I'm sure you heard of subliminal messages or unconscious or subconscious inputs like, for example, commands given to us by a hypnotiser that can trigger actions or thoughts when in the presence of the right stimulus. That or framed messages in a movie picture or something like that. Imagine that you go to the cinema and you are watching a movie that usually rolls 24 frames per second, right? If someone decides to input an image of a can of Pepsi in one of those 24 frames, the human eye won't be able to see it, but the brain will and guess what drink you will start drinking? Maybe it's Pepsi. I believe that the same is used to create wars and influence financial markets. Let's think about the Manchester Arena bombing. Why would Islamic terrorists put a bomb in a youth concert of a South American singer in Manchester – England? (And I am naturally not defending those extremist cocksuckers that should just be put inside a big bucket full of water with a heavy lid on top – killing isn't the solution for peace.) But let's think about the common denominators of the attack: terror; Islam; England and America. Now with this in your mind please keep up with my reasoning: who had just recently won the elections in America in 2017? What sort of person do you think he is? And what is one of the engines of the North America economy? Like I said this is just a thought and who am I to think I know any better than the rest; now going back to Don't Matter. – Did you see this? You heard anything about it? The Death Line? What the fuck are they talking about? Is this the end of the world? What is going to happen now? And who the fuck are these G10 people? – Don't Matter was a very simple man that thought too much of himself but whenever the world passed the land of real to the realm of science-fiction he didn't have the imaginative skills to understand it. Imagine him as a shepherd alone in the mountains of Mongolia being suddenly visited by an UFO. A true Mongolian would probably feel admired and enthusiastic about it and would definitely approach the UFO to say hi and offer them *qurut* biscuits and a cup of *airag,* whereas if something like that happened to my friend and clever Don't Matter he would probably be overwhelmed and run away scared and cackling like a crazy chicken. I never really understood why he would come to me asking all sorts of questions like was I was all-knowing. I think it had to be with the fact that I read many things about many different subjects during my life and also the fact that I had a regular habit of writing. I had that intellectual look of astute people. The reality is that reading and writing don't say much about who we are, because in the end it depends on what you read about and what you write about. For him that didn't matter. He saw me as a wise person and in a way I always tried to give him prudent answers, not that it really signified much what I told him because he would believe in me even if I told him that the Earth was in the centre of the universe; even though he is Polish he would still have faith in me. So, I did what I always do. I smiled back at him and just said: 'It's fine, Don't Matter. That's just rubbish on TV like always. Nothing is going on. The Death Line is just a name to alert people and scare them from the clever boys who can't really explain. You know how money and politics controls things, right? That's just someone planning for the future, you know? The world is not going to end, my friend. What you need to do is stop watching news; you will see that your life will become much better, trust me.' And then I turn my attention to the wooden frame on my bedsit and back to my PC with the same calm smile on my face and say one last thing before I shut up and focus on my novel: 'The G10 is group of special people here on Earth like the Avengers, you know the Avengers, right?'

He looked at me and said: 'The Avengers... yes, I know the Avengers.' And he thought about it for a few seconds and left the room towards the kitchen with a much more relaxed aura.

CHAPTER 5

Good Fortune

Back in Heaven, the big moment had come. Mary was delighted. She had the face of a child inside a candy shop. She felt like a princess after the return of her beloved knight after months away battling holy wars. Oh, her God, she was soooo happy! Finally, justice would be done! By now, with the exception of the Devil and the demons, all of them including Jesus and Mary were starting to sweat copiously. Drops of holy water could be seen dropping down from their foreheads and the grass below started to get greener as the drops touched the ground and by the end of the meeting they were standing in the middle of a very bushy area. Lucky for them, the zebras came helping and God was sitting down on the top of the big rock. He obviously had foreseen this and his love for his All Star gave him the idea of putting that big rock in that scenario. It was time to unveil the reasons for that meeting. Only the Devil and Jesus knew what God had in mind and the others had crazy hats just because they loved to make them feel special. They thought they could read minds, but they never did. God had suggested that to them during their sleep one time he had nothing better to do, then giving false hopes to his followers. It was time. God instructed a period of silence for all animals in the savannahs. Only the zebras could be heard chewing grass. 'My friends,' – he started – 'and enemies, you should all by now know the reason why we are all gathered here today,' – and he looked at Jesus and at the Virgin Mary. 'Nearly 2,000 years ago, my son Jesus created new beliefs that in a way allowed you all to exist here, today, in this moment. You know well that the reason why I never interfered was because I gave you all something called free will and with that you had the power to create your own universe. The Earth your followers have today is the reflection of your dreams and again I'm not here to judge you for it. You wished for a Heaven and for a Hell and I gave it to you. Did I not? Like I said 2,000 years ago Christianity became one of the most influential doctrines and businesses down there…Many things were stated there in those times that are part of the moralistic principles of the actual population.' God kept looking at Jesus and

Mary. Jesus had a bored aura and Mary the smile of a happy child. God carried on. 'The reason why I am here today is to discuss with all of you one of the promises in my son's book: the end of the world.' A sudden whispering invaded Africa. And God carried on. 'I would now like to say that ending the universe in not an option. The reason why is that in those times you thought you were alone in this space, but as you know now the truth is that there are many other stars in my galaxies and numerous of them have life too, and it would not be fair to them to cease existing because of promises made on Earth by one of my children.' And Jesus raised his hand wanting to talk. God did not allow it, 'Now is time to listen, my son. All of you will have the chance to express your opinions after I speak. Like I said just now, the main reason of this meeting is to discuss the end of the world on Earth, if it makes more sense for you all.' By now Mary's joy started to blur into a cloud of doubts. It was a good thing that all of them had hats because like that they were allowed thoughts without God's knowledge. Mary's mind was staring at a storm and her milky looks were turning bloody Mary. Maybe God forgot that detail when he made them the request of putting them on, or he had already foreseen what they would say or think and was just preserving himself from the attacks of the Devil and the constant prayers from his son.

'I can understand that you don't want to put an end to the universe, but what in the name of You and the Devil do you mean by discussing the end of the world on Earth? There's nothing to discuss here! You are fucking God! Jesus is your fucking son! You don't need to discuss anything here! You just need to tell us how it is going to end and that's it.' By now Mary started to melt in anger and under the 12 o'clock sun of Africa. She was now surrounded by zebras and rabbits; such was the blessed quality of her perspiration. To be fair, everyone that day with the exception of Mary knew that there would be no Armageddon happening in the year 2000.

God felt it was time to put the truth on the table and he looked straight at Mary when he said these words: 'I gave you all free will but apocalypses... it's something out of your league. Only I and my old friend the Devil have the power to end worlds, but what would be the fun in that?' The imp looked around to everyone with a devilish stupid smile on his face.

Mary couldn't take it anymore and she lost control. 'Nooooooo! You fucking asshole! No! Why? You are all fucking assholes! And you, you fucking traitor! You Judas!

I should have just aborted you!' – Looking at Jesus – 'Why did you come and fuck me that night?' – Looking at Jesus – 'I hope he gets you all in the ass for all eternity!' – Looking at the Devil – 'I hate you all! He raped me! I was raped!' She was out of control. God was about to send her to her room when she started crying and screaming, even more sounding like a crazy person, but before God had to interfere she ran away from there leaving a green trail on her path as she disappeared into the savannahs with her hat still on. No one really cared much about it because they all knew how her temper was. Eventually in a few years she would understand the reasons why vengeance wouldn't fix her heart and in a few more decades she would apologise for being so rude. In the end nothing gives us the right to be insolent to other people, does it? Life isn't about levelling scores, is it? What is life about? I'll leave that one for you readers to answer, OK? Think about it. I'm going back to my tale. Like I was saying no one really cared for Mary because they knew her too well. There was, however, someone that was seemed really concerned with her, Father Cruz. He removed his aluminium hat and made a request to God. God nodded yes with his head and Father Cruz stepped away following Mary's green trail. As he went past a small pile of wood left near the round table where the monkeys were finishing setting lunch, he grabbed a small flat piece of the giant sequoia tree and took a small knife from his pocket and started carving something on it.

God waited for everyone to chill out before he carried on talking. 'Well, my friends, I apologise for this inappropriate behaviour, but you understand how dear the end of the world was for her. Do not worry; I know she will be fine. So being let's move on because I can see the monkeys are nearly finishing preparing the table and I wish to have this matter finished before that. Like I said, there will be no apocalypse on Earth. It is, however, necessary to sort out an emergent issue; by avoiding the final judgment day we are creating a small problem. It's I'm sure to some degree fixed very soon but I would like, however, to share it with you all and hopefully together we can find a temporary solution until we come up with something better; and before one of you says it, I'll tell you that extending the size of Heaven is not an option as it might create a conflict with the balance of the rest of the universe. You have exactly the same I gave to others in other stars and that's it. Fair enough? So like I was saying, the small matter is…'; and Saint Peter raised his hand. 'You want to come over here and take my place?' said God.

Peter nodded yes and sat by Him. 'Well, my dear friends, the problem is quite simple; life on Earth has changed much in these few decades. People are becoming better with each other; the practice of good can be seen in everything they say and do down there. They are more religious; they are no doubt making us very proud up here. There is, however, a matter of concern. We are about to run out of vacancies in Heaven. We have the best builders sorting out more rooms, but it is a very slow process and in reality, we are also running out of space to build.' The Devil and the demons laughed like a group of hyenas and murmured something like: not to worry, we can help, and they laughed.

'Guys, please, can we focus here, and can you listen, please? God has spoken.' And he added more. 'Thank you, Peter, for enlightening them all about this crisis.' And Peter got off the rock and not surprisingly he went to listen to God standing near the Devil (many believe Peter and the Devil have already a side business going on involving virgin and hydro honey – maybe). 'As you have just heard, my son's plan of uniting people under the motto of love is working well; a little bit too well, I would say, but that doesn't really matter now. This is the problem and before we sit at the table to eat, we must find a solution. So now think about it and give me your opinions.'

One of the angels raised his hand and said: 'Maybe we could extend the size of Heaven?'

God looked at him and turned him into ashes. 'Anyone else not paying attention to what I just said?' All of a sudden no one wanted to talk. I wonder why. And in reality, everyone was getting hungry and you know how it works when that happens; we start getting grumpy and stop thinking straight. I also wonder if having a meeting at that time was actually a good idea. 'Anyone? Please, guys, I don't want to be the one to sort out everything in here, OK?' And he ordered the monkeys to bring them all a jug of hydro honey. 'OK, maybe that's what we all need to feel inspired.' And he raised his jug high and cheered for ideas. Everyone did the same. Jug after jug came until everyone was drunk. Idea after idea was put on the table and all of them were funny and were good, but the alcohol was doing his thing, they wanted more and more ideas and laughs and more laughs until the Devil came up with one that made everyone dream and think that it was no doubt very impressive; an idea that God would execute whilst still drunk and parting heavy with boys in the savannahs of Africa.

'I know I know I know!' said the Devil. 'Guys? You need to listen to this one! This one is amazing!' And everyone including God was enthusiastic about it. Oh, just a quick reminder of the telepathic powers of God, the Devil and Jesus – they don't work too well with hydro honey. 'Please listen!' said the Devil while petting a baby zebra in a very sensual way, 'Listen, you know the atmosphere, right?' And everyone looked a bit confused at first. The atmosphere: that shit on Earth that protects them from the vacuum in between stars and planets? Oh yeah yeah yeah. It was a generalised understanding muttering.

'And what about the atmosphere?' asked God.

'What about it? What about it? Can't you see, you drunk cocksucker? Layers! Layers! Layers!'

And there was a short silence before God spoke. 'Oh, I see what you mean, layers!' And God moved his arm up mechanically five inches at a time representing the several layers of the atmosphere.

'And it belongs to Earth. It's still in my realm,' said Jesus feeling illuminated.

'It's a good idea, is it not? said the Devil to his pal God.

'Well, for once in our lifetimes I have to say that I'm proud of you, my fallen cocksucker. Listen, guys?

Let's move on to the table and listen to what this zebra lover has to say. Let's eat.' God was the first sitting at the table and very wobbly. All the others got there too, some still wearing their crazy hats and some not; it didn't really matter anymore. 'Monkeys, thanks for your hard work! This table is amazing! Now fuck off and go look for tics or find a tree somewhere!' And there was a loud general laugh. Plus, this is what you get when you get drunk. People that get drunk don't really get how they embarrass themselves and their family and friends when they do it, especially when they are surrounded by more drunk people. I can talk for myself, what an asshole I was so many times. The more I truly believed I was funny when I was drunk the less I could see how sad and unbalanced was the image I was in fact broadcasting, but that can be a story from another book and surely how long will that tragedy be? The table was full of delicacies and God decided not to eat any animals on that occasion, so there were a few vegan and vegetarian options. Of course, Jesus Christ had also foreseen the developments of this meeting and he waited for everyone to get drunk so he could introduce a few broiled fish. I think I don't have to tell you everything else Mary had prepared for lunch because being in Heaven and having God as the master of ceremonies you should be able to imagine for yourselves. Anyway, I'll still give you a hitch of what was going on in there before I carry on with the story, giving the word back to God and the Devil. So, the beverage was simple; water (not quite sure what for), hydro honey, white and red from God's Portuguese private collection and ice wine from Canada. With best regards from our good friend the Devil. There were obviously different kinds of bread from flat bread to low GI bread with diverse kinds of olive dips nearby. Honey, pomegranates and figs spread in many sequoia bowls – Joseph could do anything with his sharp chisel; what a talented chap he was. What else? Mary loved spicy food, she thought of preparing burritos – with chilli, beans and rice, spiced tomato and cheddar, wedges, salad and sour cream. And many other foods, worth mentioning perhaps the delicious ginger beer battered halloumi with chips, mushy peas, tartar sauce and salad. Especially for the Devil and the demons she prepared candies and milk and a simple salad of chopped garlic, dressed with oil and lemon. For dessert, from other choices, there was a rich chocolate layer cake with vanilla icing and rich Madeira layer cake with pollen icing. The rest of the delicacies I'll leave for your imagination to put on top of that beautiful round table freshly cut from that giant sequoia tree. Everyone was drunk and happy. The music 'On top of the world' of the Imagine Dragons could be heard echoing from the distance all over Africa. God started hitting the table with his sequoia jug. 'Hey, cocksuckers! Your attention, please! Ahaha!' Oh, is His name he was so drunk already. He was now petting the baby zebra with the Devil. 'Hey, buddy, I love you, you know that, right? I love everyone! Ahaha! Listen, buddy, tell us more about that brilliant idea of yours; I want to do it now! What do you think? Let's do it together, hey? Ahaha!'

By now the Devil was the only one still wearing the aluminium hat and back to drinking milk, but who cared right? 'Sure! Of course!' And the Devil hit his cup only once and everyone went quiet. 'OK, my dear friends; this is my idea to sort out your issues in Heaven. It's very simple. How many layers does your atmosphere have?'

'Wait, wait let me go first!' It was God. '20! Ahaha!' he said.

'Nope,' said the Devil.

'No, really? Ahaha'!'

'And that's what you get by getting drunk.'

'Ten!' said a demon.

'Fifteen,' said one of the angels.

'Three,' said one of the saints.

'Wait, wait, I know this one; six! It's six, isn't it?' said Jesus very confident. 'I know it's six, Ahaha!'

'Nope. There are actually five main layers, you drunken fuckers! Ahaha!' Everyone laughed with the Devil, exception made to Jesus who was still thinking: – Really? No! Really?

'Yes! You can stop losing your energy with that one, OK?' And he carried on, 'Listen! There are five layers in your atmosphere but let's exclude for now the exosphere because I'm sure you don't want to take the risk of losing your souls in the emptiness. But before I carry on I would like to remind you guys that I'm well aware of the sacred rules, but nevertheless you all know that I can help you with your messy situation; plenty of vacancies where I am at.' And he blinked his eye to Saint Peter. 'Well, this is my idea: why don't you just use any of those layers to put your souls on hold until you find a more definitive solution?' Everyone one was impressed with him. Even all the animals turned their face momentarily towards the Devil from all the way from the distant savannah.

Everyone kept silent until one of the demons came out with this. 'OK, but will not the earthlings be able to see the souls floating in the air above their heads?'

'Yes, you are very right, my friend. But for that I thought also of a solution.' And he looked at God and carried on. 'Don't you have Leonardo and Raphael under your roof?'

'Yes, I do.'

'So, it's simple; you will ask them to paint the skies above exactly as the humans would see in any given day at any given time of the day. It will not be an easy task, but I'm sure they can do it.' Another moment of silence happened before all the bells in the world could be heard playing everywhere. Alleluia! Problem sorted. Now the party would carry on for a few days. Alleluia! I wonder where Mary was, if she was doing all right and if Father Cruz had found her, and what the hell he had ended up carving from that piece of sequoia tree.

CHAPTER 6

Clean Slate

I kept sitting in my living room. I lied to my friend Don't Matter when I told him that those news were just rubbish and that everything was going to be fine. Only a few times in my life I stopped being positive. I need to say that these times were troubling my mind and in front of the recent events happening on Earth and with me personally I could not avoid a very deep discomfort in my soul. What was the meaning of my dream? Why did that frame land on my lap? What did it mean? What was I supposed to do with it? I couldn't take it anymore. I decide to go out and run. I needed to clear my mind. I quickly turned off my PC and changed to my running gear, taking my phone with me. I don't usually take it with me because I hold dear the silence of that moment very much. I guess I was feeling lonely at that moment and I decided to start my runtastic app. I then made my way to the seafront and started running, taking the lower path starting by ASDA, behind Brighton's marina, following the sea towards Saltdean. – Activity starting! – said the feminine voice of my app. And as soon as I started running, she talked to me again – GPS signal lost! – I hated that shit anyway. I just kept running, focusing my brain only in pumping oxygen from my lungs to all my muscles and, as always, I found a distant point where I could keep my eyes fixed. Then I disconnect. Some people call running meditation in motion, and I think they are right. There's something very liberating when I run. I honestly have the impression that during those few miles and through that half-hour I become someone else. It feels like I turn into a superhero and who wouldn't feel better and more confident having superhuman powers? During that period I'm invincible, almost bulletproof; nothing can stop me. It's so relaxing and releasing. Running was what I really needed at that moment, but it would take me a few minutes until I managed to enter into trance mode. At the beginning my brain was fighting, searching for that ultimate understanding and enlightenment that only the concept of peace can explain. The more I tried to alienate myself from all those disturbing thoughts the more my brain kept broadcasting the image of Brighton's seafront with that angelic young woman sitting down in amity by the shore. My brain retained that image of me and her standing side by side in the perfect harmony of a love song under the most balanced oranges and pinks of the sunset. Everything was vanishing and coming back again in front of my eyes; we were there together now, then I was alone; then she was the one standing alone…I forced myself to empty my mind by focusing my attention on the sound of the steady pace of my shoes hitting the path to Saltdean but I wasn't ready to let go yet. Images of planes flying over my head tormented me like seagulls stealing fish and chips from the hands of tourists by the pier; masakra! Once again, I tried to fight it that away by focusing even more in what I was doing; focus, God damn it! But I could still listen to aeroplane engines, telephones ringing, people crying, folks laughing, more sunsets, more dawns… my head felt like a Jackson Pollock abstract painting; what a mess; tic-tac, tic-tac, tic-tac. My skull seemed made out of glass and on the edge of blowing up in millions of small pieces and in every single minor part of it there was a blurring picture revealing all my worries, fears and desires. I couldn't take it anymore. There was only one way out: running. I needed to run faster like I had never run before and so I did. I forgot I had a body and soul and become a machine. My legs transformed into testosterone fountains and the rest of my body welcomed that energy to move forward like a mustang. My heart was now my brain, and its job was only to pump enough blood to keep me alive and my eyes couldn't see more than the distant point I had marked earlier. Slowly, I braked down to a more relaxed pace. My soul was empty. I wasn't running anymore, I was levitating. All that fucking mess in my mind gave way to the shepherd through the emotion of running. Again, like many times in the past I entranced myself out of reality to a different dimension where someone just like me was a confident man and not a lost and troubled one. For the next five minutes I ran in absolute silence. Gradually the sound of the sea and the waves bathing the shore on my right hand side started building up in me, but my vision of that small distant grey dot I marked on the tall white cliff earlier was still fighting my audition. I was still in tune. For the next moments everything would still be fine. Nothing strange had happened. My father was still alive. The world was still the same. Wait. Wait! What the fuck! The distant spot on the great white wall was black, not grey! What the hell is going on here? One, two, three; just like that, like being brought back from a trance of a hypnotherapist called ignorance, I was back to realism. Every muscle of my body stopped instantly; the running machine I was had suddenly acquired

ABS brakes. 'Fuck! What the fuck!' I'm not even a person that usually swears, but this was too much. I habitually react like this when reality overwhelms me. I would like to be that person that always thinks before they talk or that says: 'For God's sake!' Or: 'Oh Lord!' But I'm not like that. When truth hits me hard and blurs my reasoning my first reaction is and will always be: what the fuck is going here!? I do apologise, but I don't fucking care! The only colour in my head was grey, all my thoughts were grey, and everything around turned into a silent shade of grey. I closed and opened my eyes a few times, trying to snap out of that freaking déjà vu situation, but it was too late. I could hear it already in the distance and just like that Boeing went over my head, coming from the north, flying towards France at an altitude less than a mile from me. I couldn't move. I stayed petrified for a while and only my sight followed the plane disappearing in the distance, but before it vanished in the horizon once again the sky shook above it and a new hole appeared and above it that strange grey colour was revealed again. From that hole another small balloon came falling gently like a feather. Hanging from it another small and unknown object was hooked. – For fuck's sake, no! Not again. I just wanted to relax my brain and have my meditation moment…I kept still and quiet looking at the object coming down less than a mile away from me. The seagulls got unexpectedly agitated and shrieked, flying away from the sea. The wind started blowing strongly to the north… it was pointless to deny it or fight; whatever had come through was meant for me. – Shit! In a matter of minutes, the balloon found me and landed safe and peacefully a few feet away from me. Hanging on to it there was another small piece of wood. Someone inside me made my body move towards that object and picked it up on my behalf. This sentence carved on it: 'Consider death as the end and the beginning of everything: the end of everything that is past and the beginning of everything that is eternal.' I read it a few times and looked at the sky above and said: 'For God's sake, can't you just tell me what the fuck you want with me? Can you stop with these crazy riddles and just tell the meaning of all this?' I was feeling lost. What training I had about faith in my past needed a quick refresh because I had forgotten it all. When you stop believing you cannot see. Faith was just like Japanese language for me or like any foreign language for the great majority of the British people. At that point I felt as if I had lost that battle, but something in my mind was telling me that I could still win the war, but what war? Strangely I felt at peace. I decided to go back to Brighton, walking back the same path I took before. Again, I was given a supernatural token. Nothing made sense anymore, but I knew now that very soon everything would be clear. The sky was a clear blue scratched with white. There were no clouds. There was no wind. Only the sea moved slowly back and forward respecting the laws of physics. Nothing else at that moment was scientific. Again, I stopped thinking and started searching for answers in my heart. In my room there was a familiar wooden frame, and in my hand I was carrying another clue. Both were connected. The wood seemed to belong to the same tree. There was someone, somewhere sending me a message and I know now that I knew already who that person was and what message he had for me. I wasn't ready yet, and that's why my soul decided to deny what my heart saw. I got home and decided to go to bed holding the two pieces of wood in my hands. I wanted to fall asleep but not to forget it; I wished to dream about it instead. Before I disconnected, I was able to listen to my friend Don't Matter and my friend Forget About Him talking about the latest news on BBC One. The last thing I heard before I unplugged was that 'the cream of mankind' was finally meeting to find   a solution for everything.

CHAPTER 7

Early spring (break)

By now all members of G10 had read God's message and as usual, whenever a matter of utmost importance was on the table it was up to the UN Secretary-General, António Guterres to organise everything. And he would do it just after finishing eating his sardines and having his bottle of red. He was having lunch and relaxing at the terrace of a very nice seafood restaurant just by the seafront at Praia Dona Ana, Lagos – Algarve; the south of Portugal. He was a happy fellow. He looked across the balcony, where one of his secretaries was sitting with one of his security detail personnel, and nodded his head using a card game sign that instructed his PA to bring him his personal business case; one of those cases with a computer screen inside and with a lot of buttons and with three different colour phones too. You know? Like those cases that people use to control the world and start nuclear wars. It was a bit out of date because nowadays, with the internet and all that most communications don't use phones anymore, but what can I say? Guterres was an old-fashioned man that liked car boot sales. I understand him well because I prefer much more to type in a poem in my old Olympia splendid 33, rather than do it on my PC. There's definitely something magical about the old days; I think that in a way technology and knowledge stole the beauty of the dark ages. It brought, for sure, necessary good, but what can I say? I'm an old-fashioned guy too. The case was now open in front of him. He looked at his coloured phones; white for Heaven, grey for Hell and black for the Mafia. In the end who rules the world, right? He caressed his phones one last time, then touched his screen on a black, white and red icon with the saying – anti-masons – underneath it. Instantly, all the other magnificent nine were alerted of the conference call. Phones, pagers, bells, you think about something else; they knew it was time to sit down and have a chat. They all stopped what they were doing and hid themselves in privacy. Whatever was going to be discussed there could only leak to the mass media after their own censorship. Everyone was online now. Their computer screen was divided in nine small round televisions. Guterres started the communication: 'Hi there, guys! How are you doing? I hope I didn't take you out of really important matters, but as you know by now it looks as if we have a square situation on our hands that needs sorting.' Everyone had their chance to confirm their attendance and to say hi to each other first and then kept in silence listening to Guterres's introduction; and he carried on: 'What do you think about this, guys? Crazy, hey!'

'Well, no doubts! I mean, it's crazy! That God and his connections! Experimental version of Xbox Ten and Lara Croft! That's amazing! I'm kind of jealous of the ego-centric bastard!' The Japanese Shinzō Abe couldn't help himself and had to make this comment.

'Yes, you are right, my dear friend. I'm kind of jealous too!' said Theresa May with a laugh.

'Well, he is God for some reason, right?' said Trump in a philosophical manner.

The rest of the magnificent ten made similar over-whelmed comments and Guterres finished this topic saying: 'No doubt he is special.' And carried on: 'Well, we can go back to this subject later, but let's just take care of the sec-ondary issues mentioned in His message.' A general Beatl-ish yeah, yeah, yeah gave way for Guterres to carry on: 'OK, so, about our Lord's message; well, at least now we have an idea of what's going on in our planet and a name to leak out for the mass media. What concerns me now is where we can meet to have a proper relaxed chat about this situation and help him sort what that Devil cunt has done to us. On the screen the rest of the glorious ten kept in silence waiting for Guterres to finish his speech. 'I don't know about you guys, but I'm actually staying in a wonderful place here in the south of Portugal and if you like the idea, I can book the whole place for us for a couple of days or for as long as we want...what do you think, guys?' Guterres was excited with this idea and obviously by now the bottle of red wine 'Passagem Grande Reserva 2009' was reaching the outskirts of his reasoning. Euphoria is now command-ing his acts. There was a moment of silence. One minute of silence for all the people that have died without expecting or deserving it in the eyes of those that think that they have any saying in what freedom or happiness is...All these ten fine examples of the human race listen to what Guterres had said. All the troubles in the world; every death we have seen when looking in the eyes of our dead; all these is what really matters for the leaders of the free world. It's not eco-nomy or monopoly of some over others; all this is now gliding inside the ten semi-gods' souls and hearts; they know they need to sit down and find a way of helping their fellow earthlings and they are going to do it; 53 54 55 and all of them shout in unison like a group of college girls: 'Spring break!' Everyone was going to the Algarve! Yay …

'How hot is it going to be in there, António?' Putin was conscious about the weather. He was afraid that if it was too warm, he could melt and smile.

'Please don't worry, number 2, this place is acclimatised, and we have single Papa mobile buggies to carry you out to the beach if you wish that, sir?'

Putin gave it a thought and nodded that he wouldn't have any trouble going with them. 'Oh, and just one other thing; I'm taking my own vodka!'

'Of course, sir!' said Guterres thinking: weirdo. And he carried on: 'All right! Anyone else has any special request?' And of course, everyone had weird shit on their mind. Maybe they were just ashamed to share it with the others or they would do it some other time, but that doesn't really matter because there were other more important issues to be taken care of. Balance; economic balance; mass trance and every concept that is really about caring for all members of society will preserve the future of mankind; equilibrium. 'No? Perfect! In that case let's all meet on the 20th. I'll have my detail picking up from Faro airport!'

'Oh really!' said one of them, 'but can we stop in Lisbon first?'

'Ahaha!' laughed Guterres, 'no need to worry, I'll have a pastry chef from Lisbon preparing you the authentic Belem pastries.' General laugh. No need to worry, my fellow earthlings, a plan is in action. The best people in our planet will take care of all of us. Well, to be fair, not all of us; I'm already enrolled in another plan. Everything in life has two poles: negative and positive. We only face troubles when we choose the limb, the ands and the maybes…

Every one of those ten human beings diligently organised their lives; the main message given to their secretaries was something like this: everything stays the same, you keep taking care of everything, but we will not be showing our faces for a few days and mustn't be disturbed under any circumstances or you know what will happen – in other words; there's plenty of people looking for work… Don't we love our bosses' recognition for all the hard work we do on their behalf? By now I was one hour into my sleep. I still had around 30 minutes of rest until I entered my first REM sleep mode and could finally have my first dreams of the night. That first dream would be the only one I would remember from that sleep. In real life I can say that it did not last longer than 15 minutes, but in the world of

dreams I think that it lasted many days. My last REM moment, probably the longest, would happen more or less at
the same time that newspapers, magazines and fresh milk
were being dropped in front of many convenience stores
around here in England and at the same time the damned
seagulls were finishing ripping off the bags of rubbish in
the same streets in the same country. From the last dream I
just recall getting out of it. I remember waking up with the
same feeling we have after making love and having an or-
gasm; – Oh, it's so good; OK, it was good; and then we
have a cigarette and everything is back to normal. It was
something great, my last dream, but then I woke up and it
was gone. But I remember well my first dream. It was
Sunday. I was five years old that day. March the 8th 1981. It
was 9:30 in the morning. It was a beautiful sunny day.
Clear blue sky. The temperature was already on 20 degrees.
I was playing alone at my grandmother's huge rear patio.
That patio was surrounded by tall old and cracked white
walls on the south and east side. On the west side a set of
five steps accessed my grandparents' kitchen and the rest of
the house. The north side had five western-style barracks
even taller than the whitewashed wall opposite it made out
of old dark grey pine wood. There were five open doors
showing only darkness inside. I wasn't afraid. I knew what

was inside. There were chickens and rabbits in one of them. There were cows and goats in another. There were pigs in another. Huge stacks of hay and corn and other sorts of food for animals. One of the doors led to the wine cellar and the rustic bathroom (a deep hole in the floor feeding the fig tree roots 20 feet away behind the barracks – lovely huge and sweet figs). There were a lot of flies singing inside that room today. I could listen to them rushing in and out as if they were doing something very important; whatever that was. There was also a fresh smell of blood coming from the inside. The last door was my grandmother's rustic oven house where she baked the most delicious plain rustic bread or with chorizo, sardines or lardoons. My favourite was the plain rustic bread drizzled with olive oil and sprinkled with yellow sugar. It was my birthday. My mother and my grandmother were preparing the food for the relatives and friends that would come to the party in a couple of hours. Well, that's what I thought was going to happen. My grandfather was sitting down on his favourite wooden seat sharpening a knife by the kitchen stairs at my level looking at me with a smile on his face. I was a happy child. My grandfather had a huge mountain of yellow sand against the south wall. I guess he put it in there to fix the cracks on the wall but maybe he didn't have the chance to do it yet. I couldn't care less. The rain, the cold, the sun and the wind had created an amazing thick crust all over it. Oh, my God, I love it. I would spend hours carving small roads and tunnels in that mountain and then play with my small metal cars; wonderful roads and even more astonishing landscapes. By the age of five I was building infrastructures and sceneries, what else did you need to be happy? 'Dad, Dad? Mum, where is Dad?' I was happy. I wasn't worried, but where was my dad? 'Mum, Mum? Where is Dad?'

I wasn't quite sure where my mum and my nanny were but I heard my mum shouting from the kitchen: 'Hey, do not bug me, boy, I'm busy and I have a lot to do!' I wasn't quite sure, but it felt she was crying.

'OK,' I said, and I carried on playing. Ten seconds after I said: 'Dad – Mum, where is Dad?' Now that I was thinking about it, the last time I had seen my father was Friday morning around 7am. He came to my bed before he went to work and very gently laid his heavy hand on my head and then leaned and kissed me; I was sleeping but I felt his fat black moustache tickling me and I think I heard him saying: 'My dear son.'

'Dad?' I needed his help. I wasn't confident building another tunnel on the north side of the great mountain. 'Dad?'

'Hey, little barrel? Be quiet. Come over here.' It was my granddad calling me. I guess he called me that when I was a little boy because I was fat.

'No! I can't now!' I answered.

'What? Come over here right now!' he shouted.

'No! I can't now, I said it already!' I was really troubled at that moment. I was just about to dig the last inch of my tunnel. I could already see the light of the sun on the other end. I needed to be very careful now or I would just collapse the whole thing and then my road would be the same with that section in that exact place.

'Come over here now, you little bastard!' And he grabbed his wooden walking stick at the same time.

'OK, OK, OK, I'm going!' And I went.

'Sit here with me and be quiet.' I sat down with him on the wooden bench annoyed and still looking at my tunnel. I hope it holds, I thought. Shit! 'Listen,' he said, 'it's about your father.' I looked at him and thought: yes, my father. I need him to help me with my tunnel, it's going break, I'm sure. And he carried on: 'You know today is birthday, right?' I nodded yes, but I didn't care, I just cared about that tunnel. 'Well, your father isn't feeling well today, and we have to be patient and wait until he is back. I'm not quite sure what's going on with him, but he needs to sleep for a while and then I'm sure he will come and help you with that, but you need to be quiet and leave him in peace for as long as he needs.'

Shit! I thought. 'OK,' I said. 'But when will he come and help me?'

'I don't know, my little barrel; he will come as soon as he feels better.'

'OK,' I answered a bit disappointed.

'Now go and play and why don't you do something else and leave the tunnel for later when he wakes up.'

I said, 'Fine!' in an angry manner and went back to the tunnel and kept excavating it gradually. I think I wouldn't be a normal five-year-old child if I didn't do exactly the opposite of grownups asked me to. Most adults are just like that that; at least I had the excuse of age on my side at that time... Fuck it! I know what I'm doing, and I don't need anyone's help! I would naturally collapse the tunnel after an hour of gently crafting and end up crying alone by great Yellow Mountain. While I was tunnelling, I could hear my mum and my grandmother talking in the kitchen. I could only hear loose words now and then and couldn't see much because the sun was opposite the entrance and from where I was watching I could only see darkness inside. I think I heard my mother cry a few times, but maybe it was only the radio on and that lamentation was coming from the Sunday mass they always listened to on the receiver in those days; they could not make it to the church and because my father was the only one driving and he wasn't feeling well they probably decided not to go; that, or maybe because it was my birthday. I don't know, I don't care. I was just worried about the passage I was building. My granddad had finished sharpening a couple of big knives and went up to the kitchen to grab a few big plastic recipients and came out again leaving all that by the big wine cellar room. He then went to another dark room and grabbed a metal hacksaw and disappeared again inside the wine cellar chamber. I heard him making a lot of surgical sounds inside, so I guess he was probably trying to save the pig's life or fix him, I don't know – that was the pig he had killed the previous day and made me watch while he was doing it as a way of building my character as a man. Perhaps the pig wasn't dead after all. I think. To be fair, I never paid much attention to the kill that day because I had already started crafting my roads on the big mountain and I was more concerned with that than watching how precisely he hit the animal's heart. I loved pigs. I loved to scratch their hairy backs and talk to them when they were alive; just the same I loved to eat them… same all, same all. It was such a beautiful day outside. The temperature was around 25 degrees. The sun was shining through a baby blue sky. The wind had stopped. Only the birds could be heard everywhere taking care of their lives. Spring was on its way, families to be made and houses to be built; in Heaven God and the Devil were playing games. On Earth the semi-gods were planning the future of mankind; the beautiful life of animals and gods. I couldn't understand why all my family was inside their caves and why my father was sleeping in the darkest room in my grandparents' house. There were no windows in that room and once you closed the door, we would find ourselves in complete darkness. Whenever I slept over at my grandparents' I was so afraid of that chamber that I couldn't even look inside it if the door was open. There was something very off with that place. My father loves it, on the other hand. I would never understand why until many years after. That room was his shame place but also his protective capsule against things I'm not yet ready to believe in. I think I will be prepared to accept it after I come out of this crazy dream I'm in now. Carrying on, another version of me was outside under the sun. My hair was blond, and my eyes are honey green. I'm wearing my Sunday best clothes, getting dirty in the sand waiting for my birthday party that will not take place. What an angel I was then. 'What time did he get here this evening?' My mother was in a controlled despair talking with my grandmother (my dad's mum) inside the kitchen while they were preparing lunch for the four or five of us, depending on my father's attendance to lunch or not... he would not come for lunch.

'It was before you got here with M.,' said my nanny.

'Was he drunk as usual?'

'No, he was not drunk. I told you already.'

'He has another woman, I know it!'

'No, Maria, he hasn't. His problem is not another woman. I told you what his   problem is.'

'I don't believe it! That's just an excuse you invented to justify his alcohol addiction, his whores and his war traumas! What does a man do during two nights without showing up at home? He doesn't care about me or his son, just his whores!'

'No, Maria, why don't you believe me? I told you before that his problem is the same my father had. I saw it in his eyes yesterday when he crossed my doorstep and went to the room. It wasn't him, Maria. It was not my son, the man that I saw this morning. Why don't you trust me? We need to take him to Madame Celeste's house today when he wakes up before it's too late.'

'I don't believe in what you're saying! You are just defending him because he is your son!' My mum was desperate. She didn't know in what to believe anymore. Maybe my grandmother was right. Maybe there was something wrong with my father; something outside the realm of the living.

'No, Maria. You need to believe me. He is my son and I'm not defending him, I'm just telling you what has to be done for him, Maria, before it's too late… before he follows the same path as my father…' and my grandmother started crying. My mother felt her pain and joined her crying in a chorus. My grandfather went into the kitchen a few minutes after carrying a large recipient with different cuts of the pig and with his hands full of blood. I guess he did not manage to fix the pig. Either that or the animal had no use of those organs and had turned into some sort of Mary Shelley's Frankenstein. I heard them talking for a while; I heard my father's name and my name. They whispered many more words that I was not acquainted with yet. He came out again and went back again to the operation room.

I was so afraid. I could see the tunnel collapsing. I knew it was going to happen. And it did. Shit! Shit! Shit! Shit! And I started crying like the baby I was. If someone had told me at that age that we end up getting what we create in our minds I would have thought that everything would be fine instead of keeping creating failing scenarios. I closed my eyes and turned my back to the kitchen and moaned for more than an hour waiting for someone to come to my rescue or notice me. I felt lonely. I felt what children should never feel: indifference. My sadness was about to turn into anger when I heard the manly balanced and gentle voice of my father: hey, my little artist...what's going on here? I looked up and there he was: my father. The sun was just above his head; six feet tall, wide shoulders; my own God, my superhero, my dad. 'Dad!' I jumped three feet high whilst turning my body towards him in a blind leap of faith; I knew he would catch me and hold me tight against his fitted body and he did. I was safe now. I was so happy. My mother, my grandmother and my grandfather were standing at the kitchen doorstep watching us with a dubious look on their faces. There was something fearful and hopeful in their eyes, I still don't know why...my father would never hurt me and they knew that, and yet they didn't believe it enough to allow him alone with me at that moment. He knew they were watching us, but he didn't care about it. He was there for me and for him. Both of us needed that hug. Both of us needed to push our anger away. My father smelled of alcohol and cigarettes and something else... I didn't care. I wasn't there to judge him, and he wasn't there to judge me. I guess that is what love is; acceptance without judgments.

'Ah, my little M. ... how are you, my dear son? What's is going on? Why were you crying here alone and by yourself? What happened in there? Why are you crying, my little man?' His voice had that balanced dream tone of a hypnotist. His smile had no teeth, but his eyes had the shine of stars. I was still crying but it was now from happiness, not from sadness. I love you so much... I thought. I love you so much...he thought. I pointed my finger to my collapsed tunnel and he said: 'Uau! Look at that! Amazing! You did all that by yourself?' He asked me while looking at the roads and the other tunnel I had built.

'Yes!' And I jumped to the floor and took him with me around the yellow mountain showing him my constructions. I felt like an engineer and an architect at the same time. I felt proud of myself because my father was delighted with me: it's such an amazing feeling when love blurs disbelief away and sadness stops having a conceptual meaning, is it not? My father leaned closer to my work and grabbed one of my plastic modelling tools and did some minor works to get my roads in perfect condition. He then looked at the collapsed tunnel and looked at me:

'So, what happened here?' I shrugged and smiled at him. 'I see. Come here with me.' He asked me in a very professional manner. 'Look; look at this tunnel you made here.' And I looked. 'Can you see in what angle you carved it in the mountain?' I looked to the place he marked with his finger and I understood instantly his point; the place I had chosen to carve the second tunnel was too close to the edge and too shallow. The lower part of the tunnel was doomed to break from the beginning. 'Do you understand now why it collapsed, my little artist?' I said yes with a disappointed look. 'Hey! What's going on, my little engineer? Don't put that face, OK? Where there is a will there's a way!' I didn't understand quite what he meant with that but somehow, I felt assertive all of the sudden. 'We can fix this!' he said in an absolute confident manner. 'Go to the kitchen and ask your mum for a big glass of water. Then ask your grandmother for a card tube from a toilet roll; I'm sure she has one about to finish, and on the way, ask my father for a one sheet of his newspaper. Tell him to go have a shower and change his clothes because we need to go visit someone after lunch and his bloody clothes won't help my cause. Did you understand everything?'

'Yes.' I didn't know what his plan was, but I felt like a little man given adult duties. I went and collected what he asked me and told my grandfather to get ready to go out. 'Here!' I was excited.

'OK. Well done! I'm proud of you. Now let's fix this.' I watched him as he excavated a small volcanic crater on the lower part of the mountain and poured the glass of water in it. After he cleared the obstructed road where the tunnel had collapsed, and he flattened one side of it he placed the cardboard tube in place and rolled in the plastic my grandfather gave me. He was doing this and looking at me and explaining all steps of the process, making sure I was not only seeing everything he was doing but also understanding, so I would know how to sort out issues like that in the future. 'And now you grab this wet sand with your hands and shape it anyway you want over the cardboard structure.' And finished it making it look it like that section of the mountain had been there for millions of years; after he cleaned the road on both sides and looked up at the sun and then at me he said: 'Now, let's allow the elements to work out their mysteries and after lunch your tunnel will be perfect; see, no need to cry; everything is fine.'

'I love you, Dad.' He smiled and took me by his hand, and we went to celebrate my birthday. After lunch I would be introduced to a new and strange world where a lady talking to imaginary people lived in a very small isolated house in a village 30 miles away from us. The house was in a rural pine tree area and was surrounded by barking dogs and frisky cats. I remember a dark room full of mystery; they were dressed in funny costumes. A place stinking of mould, decomposing matter, roses, pine, incense, other unknown fragrances, olive oil and burning candles; a strange, frightening and mysterious place. I'll get back to this point in a few chapters. Now let's allow the words to marinate for a while so they get a full and transcendent meaning. I carried on my nirvana dream holding two strange pieces of wood in my hands; planes kept vaporising in the skies. Our world was changing. Tension was building in the human hearts. Scientists couldn't find any answers for the phenomena; frustration was taking place; religions were radicalising; economy was now a tempest sea. Nearby, in space the last satellites flying around the earth could only show the perfection of Leonardo and Raphael's paint job on the atmosphere; what the fuck is going on here? Selfishness was taking over. Manchester bombings or Lollapalooza festivals were small compared to what would come; but not to worry; G10 was taking care of the final details for their early spring break in the south of Portugal and they would find a way, right? I wonder what's going on in Heaven.

CHAPTER 8

Under the Tree of Knowledge of Good and Evil

I'm not quite sure if I should say what was happening around the round sequoia table. Let's say that the final details about the Devil's idea to sort out the shortage of vacancies for good souls in Heaven would have to be settled a few days after the party. His idea was good. But for how long could God accommodate the souls of all living things in the different layers of the atmosphere? Yes, let's not forget that just because Christians believe that the human race is the only one with a soul worthy of reincarnation, that does not mean it's true. In the universe every atom is eternal. Everything has a soul. Why would the sun exist if it did not have the understanding of its role in the balance of planets? Soon enough, after a universal headache God would realise how fragile, ephemeral and malicious the Devil's plan had been. But you know how selfish God is, right? He is in many ways like a lot of us; he doesn't like to apologise and instead of manning up and finding a solution for what he allowed to happen he would eventually (maybe) pass the hot potato to someone else's hands. Perhaps we are all Gods in the end.

Mary was 30 minutes ahead of Father Cruz. That might not seem much at first, but it all depends where she decided to stop to cry, regret or plot alone against both her Lord and her Son. The distance between them could last for an eternity if she decided to walk forever and I need to say that she was much younger than Father Cruz and she never needed any stick in her life to walk or for having a child. On the other hand, Cruz had been canonised late in his life, so speed was not his best feature, but in his God's name he was a true believer and he would walk forever if he had to. Good thing that Maria had decided to think about her life under the tree of knowledge and that Jerusalem was just on the top corner of Africa and that also God's version of the Earth was on a very small scale. So, let's say that about two hours after Father Cruz left God's parade and followed the green path left behind by the Virgin's holy tears, he found her. From the distance it looked as if she had a sad expression, but she was instead disguising the face of a hurt woman plotting against the root of her sadness. Mary was no carrier of hope in this moment under that tree; she was just another woman angry at the unfairness of a world still commanded mainly by ruthless and uncaring men. She had her aluminium hat on, by the way, and she was picking petals of a Blackfoot Daisy as she was saying the following: 'Fucking asshole! Fucking child molester! You think I didn't feel it? You fucking raped me, you fucking asshole! And the little bastard! Of course, he would stay on your side! Fucking assholes! Damn you all together!' And she picked another daisy. 'Ah! But this shit is not going to end like this!' And she carried on saying and wishing even more blessed things. In the end all saints can be reduced to regular people, right, '...for dust thou art; and unto dust shalt thou return...'? Every mother was once a Virgin Mary in potency and will one day, if loved in life, become a Holy Mother. There was so much resentment in her heart that she would probably destroy all the daisies under the tree. Luckily for the plants Father Cruz had caught up with her. He decided to give her a few more moments alone and stayed hidden behind a few bushes about 50 yards away. Everyone should know that when a woman says that she needs to be alone most of the times it just means that what she wants in reality is more attention but not always, sometimes being alone is what she really needs. I believe that most of the arguments between couples occur because no one really knows what goes on inside their heads...does she really want to be alone...does she not? What a daisy life we live in. Cruz was carving a few words on his small sequoia slate whilst observing the Virgin from the distance. She was sitting down with her back against the tree; it had no apples and the snake was ambushing rodents somewhere else. He could see from her beautiful figure only diminished by the ridiculous aluminium hat on her head. Cruz was a very simple and wise man and we know how the simplest people can say so much with just a word, don't you agree? You put a poet talking about life and the most amazing words full of mixed feelings and images, symbols and rhythms come to life but you put a shepherd on a hill looking at his flock; you give him a dog, a Cornish pasty and a warm cup of tea; asking about life and he will probably genuinely smile and say that life is simple and beautiful because ultimately we are the creators of the world we live in. Father C. was good with people because he was firstly a good man. When you sow well you can only harvest respectability and so on. It seemed she was calming down. Mary stopped picking up petals. Both her heart and soul had purged most of her troubling ideas. It was time for Cruz to show himself and he did. Slowly, in the same way we try to walk past a sleeping lion he approached her and sat down on a small flat rock a few feet away from her. She never saw or heard him coming. She was absorbed in her thoughts and he kept in silence carving his small text on the piece of wood waiting for her to come out of her trance in her due time. No one likes to be pulled out of a good dream, whatever her dream was now; a few minutes after she came back to reality and saw him carving the piece of wood in a silence only broken by the noise of his small knife engraving letters turning into words and into sentences and into meanings.

'I had a dream with you, Father Cruz,' said Mary in an excessively confident and controlled manner. 'But I saw you with a different piece of wood,' she carried on, 'it's not going to happen, is it? My husband changed his mind, did he not? Can you tell me what's his plan now, Father Cruz?'

'I will tell you everything, my lady, as soon as soon as you relax your heart a bit more.' And he took a small bottle of hydro honey and a slice of angel cake from his bag and gave it to her. 'Oh, you can remove that hat now because I'm pretty sure that no one will be able to read any minds at that lunch at this point.'

Mary removed her hat and smiled back to him saying: 'I was imagining the same   by now.'

'Just relax your little heart, Lady Mary, and we have all the time in the world to talk about the future.' They sat down together for a while in peace while she drunk the beverage and had her cake. Cruz finished his engraving and put the slate back inside   his bag.

'OK. Thank you, Father Cruz, for coming after me and for being here with me. You are a good man and a worthy saint.'

'Oh, sweetheart, there's no need for that; you know how I admire you and how I understand your resentment.' Father Cruz was preparing her mind for his monologue.

'Yes, I know you do, Father. Please carry on. You are going to tell me about my dream, are you not?'

'Yes,' he added and followed by taking his small pocket Bible from his bag and opened it on a specific page and he read a few lines before he carried on with his own thoughts: ' "Forgive us the wrongs we have done, as we forgive the wrongs that others have done to us." ' And he opened another page: ' "For I know the thoughts that I think toward you, says the Lord, thoughts of peace and not of evil, to give you a future and a hope." ' Naturally both Cruz and Mary knew the Bible by heart, but there's something immensely special and rewarding when you read lines from a real palpable book, is there not? It's like reading an eBook or a hard cover book. Nothing will ever surpass the fragrance of a new or an old book, will it? Mary heard Cruz and kept silent. He closed the Bible, keeping it in his hands and looked Mary into her soul and carried on his monologue. 'Well, my dear Maria, before I tell you what your husband and the Devil decided to change about the end of world for the earthlings, I would like to tell you about a dream I had a night ago.'

'Oh, you had a dream, too?' inquired the Virgin with interest and surprise. It's not very common for gods, semi-gods, saints and so on, having dreams; they don't need to dream, they are more on the plane of listening and do but every so often, perhaps due to reminiscences of their past lives, they dream sometimes.

'Yes, I did,' answered Father Cruz, nodding his head slowly, affirmatively, for a few seconds bringing back his unclear memories of it. 'I was here with you talking about a dream I had.' Small pause and deep breath and he carried on again in a very tranquil and introspective manner. 'Was telling you how your Husband and the Devil had found a way of not ending the human race. It was a very stupid idea sown by the Devil about creating something called the Death Line on the first layer of Earth's atmosphere, but somehow it had been accepted by all, except you and me. In a way my dream was telling me that the end of the world would come after all. All that you most wanted would eventually happen, not in 2000 but in 2020. We were sitting exactly where we are now. We talked about this matter for a while and then we were both transported by a phoenix to the troposphere and the bird flew around the planet a few times.' He paused for his thoughts again and looked around and then to the sky and spoke still very calmly but with concern. 'I could see only one colour, Mary; the Devil's favourite colour, Mary. There were no shades of blue, white, green or brown, Mary; there was only his shade: grey. I felt and still feel very worried. What did that mean? I saw you once again in my dream just before I woke up in my bed at the saint's monastery. Before we spoke one last time again in my dream, again here where we stand, I saw myself flying again on a phoenix and dropping two objects on to Earth two different days. I saw where they landed and who picked them up and I know now the reasons why, Mary. My dream ended here, exactly here where we stand, with us trying to find a solution for all this mess and I was sure that you didn't want an apocalypse anymore. We were chatting when God interrupted me with a message about a very important summit and I woke up.' And he went quiet.

Mary was processing the words he had just said and naturally she had a few questions and so she went after a while: 'I see. What made you feel I did not wish for a Judgment Day anymore, Father Cruz?'

'Well, like I said, my lady: it was just a dream, but you recognise surely how good I am with people, don't you? And why would you stand here under this tree if not for a new start? And does a new start have to mean the end of an entire race? Is nirvana not a spiritual endeavour? And are the earthlings to blame for being free and inventive? And in the end of all things who allowed them the ideas and the concepts?' Father Cruz could go for hours talking about reasons to save the human race. He loved them very much. Imagine someone that starts working in a new business, doesn't matter what trade, just imagine you being told what to do without having any sort of follow up or feedback after. How could we become better like this in whatever we do? Cruz's goal was to point out that maybe the employees were not to blame in the history of Christians but the mentors instead. Don't you agree? How can we be better if we are not given the right tools and the right support to achieve perfection? How many of us have been planned training hours and in the end were just dropped inside the lion's den having to learn our own ways out of the pit? Are we to be blamed if we do mistakes? Don't think so, but you think about it; going back to the tree; Mary listened to Cruz's questions and feelings and gave it some thought before responding:

'So, you had a dream that is in the end what's going to happen, is it not?' Cruz nodded affirmatively. 'And you say that they end up provoking the end of the world of earthlings after all, so why would I do anything to change that?' And she went quiet, looking at the small pool of water in front of her. Father Cruz allowed her to think about it for a while. He knew, somehow, that Mary never wished for an end of the world and that she was in the end just like many women in this world; human beings considered inferior and that can be easily manipulated by men's twisted minds. Society is a very cruel concept. Even nowadays how many countries treat their women as the simple vehicle of continuity and assign them with the role of education and housekeeping? I mean, how long ago was England still paying lower salaries to women just because they were women; crazy, right? But that's the world we live in. Maybe the solution isn't the eradication of an entire race and just a part of it? Some people are just too empty or low moralistically, but the truth is that the great majority of men still bully their wives and treat them as objects. Am I wrong here? How many times have you imposed yourself sexually upon your wife? How often do you help her with the tidying? How many times have you prepared meals for her or your children? How many times have you shown your face at school for a parents' meeting? How often do you praise her? How many times do you give a smile or a hug? And what is your excuse, work, being tired, and football game, what? How many times have you tried to put yourself in her shoes and see how heavy those are? Cruz sees all that in her and that's why he was confident that she never wished for any wrongs for human beings, she was just another bullied woman; poor her that had the sun of the Big Bang as her husband. Cruz was searching in his soul for the right word to click her out of that trance she was given the day Jesus was sown inside her; in a way he was travelling his unconscious moments finding the word that would then make her travel her own and find the right answer and he found it:

'Joseph,' he said; the billion-dollar word. Instantly Mary snapped out of her trance. She then looked at Cruz and up at the sky where flamingos were just passing by. She looked and absorbed all that colour of love and closed her eyes and dived back 2,000 years searching for an answer. She stopped her regression in the day she couldn't hide her pregnancy anymore and Joseph discovered she was pregnant. She was now looking at his face. There was peace in his face. He trusted her. But how could he? The great majority of men would react like that. I was understood and he respected me. He treasured me. He helped me so much and he was happy for that child inside me knowing that he wasn't his. He didn't even know I was still a virgin at the time. What does this mean? He wasn't even a saint at the time. What is this? What word am I looking for? And she whispered several times: 'Love, Love, Love, Love…' and then she opened her eyes and looked at Father Cruz and said: 'You are right, Father; there is still hope for this world because I'm sure there is love in their souls, right, Father?

'Yes, my lady,' he answered with a smile in his face.

'So, Father, let's talk more about your dream and your idea to fix what my husband and the Devil have created this time. Do you think they are still there enjoying themselves?' This was a rhetorical question, naturally. The summit would last for very long. Cruz gave her another smile and then he breathed deeply, preparing to put all cards on the table and with the help of Mary find a solution to fix what others had screwed.

'Oh yes, I'm sure they are. And I was thinking, my lady; I don't know how your Husband set up this day; if we are only going to have sun or will there be night as well...'

'Oh! My Husband, damn Himself! I forgot to ask too.' said Mary. 'Why don't we start walking back and we talk about your dream on the way? I'm sure no one will take care of tidying up after them in that place and those monkeys are probably drunk too. Let's go and take a few more monkeys with us. I've seen a big group a couple of miles away from where the lunch was taking place and I'm positive they will come with us and help.

'Oh yes, definitely! All the monkeys love you very much and they are so easy to deal with.' Cruz stood up and led his Lady to the green path back to the summit.

'Thanks, Father.' And they started making their way back. It was now around 4pm and at the summit the picture was wild. Everyone, including monkeys and zebras, was drunk. God had by then made a vinyl player and a few dozens of old records appear on the table and he told one of monkeys to be in charge of the music and he was. At this moment, Newsboys – 'God's not dead' was playing. The Devil was resting on the floor against God's rock, hugging a couple of virgins that he swiped in the meantime, drinking milk and smoking some very powerful pot (it smelled like Manali West's Nova OG); God was dancing with a lady monkey and saints were dancing with demons. A few of the last where riding zebras up and down the hill. Everyone was happy. Even the zebras were enjoying a few hard slaps on their asses: 'Come on, baby! Give it too! Come on! There you go! That's it!' And so you know I'm not lying, and the animals were enjoying themselves very much, both monkeys and zebras created their own queues and were taking turns either to dance with God or to be ridden by a demon or by a saint occasionally. The reality is that the zebras preferred demons more than saints. The common holy crap: 'Come on, sweetheart, let's go. Do you mind me riding you? Am I hurting you? Is it OK like this?' And so on, wasn't really impressing those zebras. Sometimes a nice slap on the ass and a good vibrant ride is just what they need, right? What a scenario that party had become! By now there were monkeys doing monkey dances on the table and throwing cakes to everyone. There was food scattered all over the table and on the floor; empty bottles of hydro honey and mugs redecorating the canvas. I think that at this point only someone like Claude Monet could create a painting that made any sense and could deliver some sort of beauty to that picture. What an impressive work of art that would be! Mary and Father Cruz had just left the tree of knowledge and Mary was now interested in hearing about the dream. She felt that a new opportunity had been put in her path. With Cruz she had now the chance to become the true hero of Christianity. She would fix the world. She wasn't quite sure of how to do it and even Cruz was kind of lost, but together they will find a way. M was still dreaming and the G10 were finalising last hour details for their early spring break. What a wonderful world we live in!

'About your dream, Father, what did you send to that man on earth, and why him? What do you think of that? Who is he? Is he one of the marked ones? Do you know his number?' asked the Virgin as they walked.

Cruz thought about it for a while before saying something and then he added: 'His number is PT/08/03/1976/08:00.'

'This number never prayed in my name, that's for sure.'

'I'm not quite sure, my lady. He is definitely important for us, but I haven't been able to make the connection.'

'Oh, I see. He has prayed in my name and my Husband's many times. And what was is his father's number?' asked Mary. Women have this brilliance of quick thinking, don't they? Whilst Father Cruz was still trying to find the true meaning of his dream within the dream, the pieces of wood he had carved and in the use of M in this riddle, Mary was already linking dots and opening other doors that could lead to a why; why him?

'His father's number? You will have to give me a few seconds because I left the book of my devotees at the monastery, but not to worry; I don't remember all their files but I know all their numbers by heart; OK, so his father's name is António and his number is PT/05/04/1950/08:00 and I'm afraid I do not recollect more of his data but I know this number prayed in my name many times.' And he went silent trying to make a connection.

Mary picked up from where he had stopped: 'Yes, this number prayed regularly, both in my name and in my Husband's; and they were born at the same time...There's definitely a possibility in here, Father Cruz; I'm sure you know what sync happenings mean and the potential they have, especially when within the same blood line?' Mary stopped and looked Cruz in the eyes. 'You know what that means, right?'

Father Cruz nodded yes and explained what that meant so all of us could understand as well. 'That means that one of them has the potential to be either a saint or a demon, but regardless of that these two numbers can communicate between parallel worlds. All they have to do is find the right universal frequency.'

'Exactly,' said Mary.

'So now all we need to find out is why both of them are so important for us.'

'Definitely. I'll collect my book soon as we get back to Heaven and we will know then.' And they carried on talking more about all that mess.

CHAPTER 9

The house in the woods

I guess that this was the quietest happy birthday party I ever had or would ever have. Apart from the moment by the end of lunch when all of us cheered my name and I was given six candles to blow, only the noise of the cutlery cutting meat, mouths chewing food and distressed sighs, no more words were said. I was the only one looking at their faces and noticed worries in all their looks. Maybe because it was my birthday, they decided just to drop their attention on me. I wasn't sure, but my father stamped another smile on my face when he got up from the table and went to grab my birthday present. Uau! I felt so happy. He gave me a football – Adidas. Oh my God! I felt the luckiest child in the world; an Adidas! Until that day the few times I had seen one like that had been on TV and a few other times my father took me to watch (live) his favourite team in the universe, Benfica. It was funny, because I was just a child and I shouldn't be aware of things like that so early in my life, but the fact is that when my father gave me that ball I could see in his eyes that we would not go out to play in the patio. He had that look saying it is time to go. I didn't know where, but I was going to find out very soon. I was absorbed in dreams with my ball and I was listening to the things they were saying but I wasn't really paying attention to it.

'Shall we go?' declared my father in a very calm and confident manner whilst looking at everyone.

'And what about him?' asked my mother tilting her head in my direction.

Before my father said something, my grandma added: 'He is just a child. He's OK and doesn't understand anything; just give him one of his comic books and he will be fine.' How wrong you were, my dear grandmother; if you only knew how information imprints in us and stays there, latent, waiting for future clicks, waiting for the right stimulus to bring   it out.

My grandfather drank the rest of his wine and got up from his chair and said: 'Well if it's go, let's go then!' He loved sitting his ass inside a car. Sometimes I think that in another life he had servants taking him to places. He felt so important inside my dad's car; front seat; waving to everyone, like a proper king, in the village, as my father made his way into the house in the woods. I was sitting down at the back between my mother and my nanny reading one of my favourite comic books, *The Lone Ranger*. I had dozens of comic books. My parents bought me a few, but it was mainly my grandfather who offered them to me. It was the best way he found to keep me quiet every morning my grandmother was at the local open market selling their own produce of fruit, vegetables, plants and flowers, eggs and sometimes live animals like chickens, rabbits and even goats. She would stay there all morning at her stand trying to make money and my grandfather would stay at on the local *tasca* the whole morning drinking glasses of red wine and eating pork scratchings, marinated pork heart, salted cod, fried sardine and other typical nibbles. So, every morning before he joined his pals inside the *tasca* he would buy me a couple of comic books at the newspaper agent nearby. It's funny how, nowadays, whenever I need some time alone in order to clear my mind, I go and choose pubs and other crowed places to do it. Maybe that ability came from those mornings with my granddad. He would sit me on a table in a middle of men getting drunk, talking about football, politics, religion and women. He would always offer a meat sandwich and a bottle of J2O or a small glass of red depending on his mood and never on mine. I was just a boy, so I was OK with whatever he gave me. He was the adult, so I guessed he knew better; and then as soon as I started my reading my brain would transport me to a different universe where the land was arid and hot and the smell of horses, sweat and gunpowder would invade all my senses; my attention would only be interrupted whenever someone came inside or left the *tasca;* and don't ask me why a place like that in the centre of Portugal had typical western saloon doors, but that doesn't really matter now. I had a cowboy comic book in my hands, and I was sitting on the back seat of my parents' car. A brand-new midday blue 1.2 Toyota Corolla. It took my dad about one hour to get to that house in the forest. He drove mainly on dirt roads and tough pine and eucalyptus lands. He never asked my grandmother for directions, so I guess it was not his first time going there. Maybe he first travelled to that place when he was my age. I never asked him that question. After an hour he stopped in front of a small house surrounded by dogs barking as if the Devil was around. It was an old stone house that was being claimed back by the forest. The side walls were covered by blackberry bushes and there were very old cracking apple and plum trees in the middle of that messy scenario. The dogs were chained to old and rusty metallic barrels. The house had one door at the centre and one small window at each side. That creepy picture grabbed my attention from my book and transported me to other horror books I had in my collection. 'Creepy,' I said with a smile in my face interrupting that silent moment that took over everyone inside that car. I was very excited. I couldn't control myself. 'Where are we? Where are we going? Why are the dogs barking? Why is this place so old? Is this a witch house? Creepy!' And with this last sentence I touched a sensitive subject.

'No. Don't be a fool. It's not a witch house! It's the house of friend of mine that, that…' My nanny was taking her time to find the right words; my granddad decided helping her in that moment, so he said this with a laugh:

'It's nothing, you little bastard! You are reading too many books! Come on, let's go outside and see what's going on with these dogs! Come on!' And he opened the door and I rushed outside with him. I loved spending time with him. He was a bad person, but he loved me very much and always treated me like a little prince. My father was in silence still holding the wheel. My mum was behind him with her eyes closed. My mum was a very religious human being. But she had doubts about the true reasons behind my father's regular disappearing; sudden changes of mood and specially for talking with invisible people. My mum could accept traumas of war, but she would just presume all the rest to alcoholism. Time would show us all the truth.

'Shall we go, my son? Shall we go, Maria?' My grandmother meant business time.

My mum was the first answering: 'I don't care! It's up to him. I don't even know why we are in here! This is all bullshit!' My mum was angry.

'Maria? That doesn't help, my daughter.'

'That doesn't help? So what helps then? And you are not my mother!' My mum said this to my nanny and opened the door and went outside and called me: 'M.! Come over here! Leave the dogs alone! And you, what are you doing? I don't want my son near those dogs!' And then she whispered to me: 'I don't want my son in this place.'

My granddad gave her that 'what a weirdo' look and carried on petting the dogs that had calmed down by now. My dad was watching the scene from inside the car and was still holding the wheel. 'António; my son, we need to go.'

'I know,' he answered with a deep breath. He followed by opening the door and went outside with my nanny. At the same time a curtain was closed in one of the windows of the house hiding a short figure of a woman. It was Madame Celeste. Now she was sure that my father would go inside. The first demon had given up and allowed him to leave the car. Outside, my grandfather had made friends with the dogs, no wonder why, he brought with him a bag of pork scratchings. I guess this wasn't his first time in that place. I was with my mum halfway between my car and the house near some old roses that were half-covered by tall grass. It looked as if everything in that place was half-something. The dogs were now dead on the floor; white foam was coming out of their mouths. My grandfather and my grandmother were joyful with that. What was going on? It was my dream. My dream was suddenly turning into a nightmare. In my bed in Brighton spasms took over my rested body. I started shaking and sweating as if I had a sudden change in my body temperature, but I wasn't ready to let go of that dream. I needed a connection. I wanted to understand why I had been given those relics; in my dream, the shapes of objects were shaking too. Everything was hanging by a very thin string. A simple doorbell or a sound alert in my phone could snap me out of it and how often can we go back to the same dream? – Once in a lifetime. A few cats now leaked the clear white blue foam from the dog's lips and very soon they were dead as well. A sudden silence was broken by my grand-parents laughing as they entered that house where only a very shy dark yellowish medieval light could be seen glowing in the back room. I was now like a little sausage inside a hot dog roll made of Mum and Dad. The three of us were watching the animals dying but none of us had any feelings about it. I remember hearing my father's voice with the same weighty, well-adjusted and confident tone. 'Let's go?' My mother's attitude had changed. She wasn't upset anymore. She looked subdued by a greater energy. She looked entranced; my father grabbed my mum by one hand, held me with the other and walked us through the dying animals. They were not dead yet. They were still choking in their own fluids. A final wheezing sound could be heard coming out of their guts as we approached the entrance door. The outline of every shape in my dream, including ours, was chronically shaking. The recurrence was getting shorter. Something was about to change. Our figures fast forwarded inside the dark room. Silence took over. One minute of silence honouring the spirit world; deep breath; 1, 2, 3, 4, 5, 6, 7, 8 (strong shake in this dream), 9, 10, 11, 12, 13, 14, 15, 16, 17, 18, 19, 20, 21, 22, 23, 24, 25, 26, 27, 28, 29, 30, 31, 32, 33, 34, 35, 36, 37, 38, 39, 40, 41, 42, 43, 44, 45, 46, 47, 48, 49, 50, 51, 52, 53, 54, 55, 56, 57, 58, 59,

60. It was a small room with a single bed against one of the walls, one small round table with a big soup plate on it and a black book and one free chair; the other one was taken by Madame Celeste and four chairs against the opposite wall where I sat with my mum and my grandparents. A big and old chest of drawers was against the other wall. On the top of it there were several wooden photo frames with different people in all of them. The poor light didn't allow me to re-cognise anyone. There was also a different oval-shaped plate and small gold medals with engraved saints on it, a bottle of olive oil, a small plate with ignitable wicks like those from tea light candles, a few small praying leaflets and a few bags with different kinds of herbs. The room had a new scent for me. I would sense that smell many other times at my parents' house in the future. Why was I having this dream? Why do we dream? Is it just to defragment our soul, a journey of learning through our unconscious mo-ments or a chance to see the future, or none of them? Whatever reason made me be there with my family in that moment was about to disappear. In Brighton my body wouldn't take the pressure for much longer. Fuck it! I need to make connections! There we were. My father sat down in front of her with that strange small fat woman in silence looking at her. She looked at my grandmother and asked

her with a very balanced light tone: 'Did you bring it?' I wonder how my grandmother spoke with her earlier because none of them had phones at their homes and there was no way any of them would have the time to meet each other and arrange that reunion. Something wasn't right there. Of course, this was just a dream but there was definitely complicity between the two of them.

'Yes,' answered my nana whilst taking from inside her bag the shirt my father dressed for the last two nights he had disappeared. She handed it to her – she grabbed it, looked at it and then smelled it; another dream shake. I was sitting down between my mum and my grandmother looking at my father and that woman with a wow face. – Amazing, I thought. I never thought there were people whose job was to smell other people's clothes, but fair enough. After smelling it she looked at my father and followed by pouring olive oil inside the plate and dropped a few ignitable wicks floating on it using a match to light them up. I guessed it was because it was too dark in that room. That new light gave the chance of seeing a little bit better the objects and images on the top of her chest of drawers. Everything was still a bit blurry so I couldn't actually recognise any of the faces. What I was able to see was that every single wooden furniture item inside her bedroom belonged to the same kind of tree. It looked like some exotic wood from another continent because I was acquainted with the different kinds of timber natural to Portugal and I'm sure I had never seen wood with those shades of reddish, brown and grey swirling veins. My attention was then pulled back to Madame Celeste when she started whispering what sounded like a religious prayer or enchantment. My dream shook heavily. I felt like a magnet between my mum and my nanny. It was as if both of them were battling for my body. Madame Celeste's wicks started moving by themselves on that plate as if a calm sea was under attack, an Adelaide storm. Madame Celeste had her eyes closed; she shuddered a few times on her chair and her voice went from calm and silent monastery tone to harsh and strident a few times until time slowed down. I could still see the wicks floating on the oil, but everything was in slow motion.

'Hi António.' It was Madame Celeste talking to my father. There was something wrong. It wasn't her and or her voice. It sounded like a clerical masculine voice – fuck! What the fuck is going on here? No! No! Fuck, no! – Back in Brighton I was still sleeping but I had started muttering these words. I was grabbing both the photo frame and the wooden slate with all my strength. I needed to stay there a bit longer. So far, I hadn't been able to make the connection. I needed something stronger; a crucial clue that would stick in my mind after I woke up. 'You know why you are here, right?' she carried on. My father was calm as if everything happening in there was part of the real world. Somehow, I felt that he belonged in that world, but why and how?

'Hi, Father. Yes, I know why I am here.'

'Your safe has been cracked, António; the time has come for you to choose your fate.'

'Yes, I know. But he is too young to understand, Father.' Oh God! What the fuck is going here? With whom is my father talking? And who is too young, me? Are they talking about me? I couldn't hold my dream anymore. Everything shook tremendously and every shape in that dream dusted away.

'He will be exactly the same age you are now when the time comes. 8, 8, 8, 8.' It was the last thing I heard echoing away when my body jumped like a spring back in my bed in Brighton. I immediately dropped the two pieces of wood on top of my drawer and grabbed my pen and my notebook. I wrote down the words dream, time comes, 8, Father and wood. I looked at it and waited for some sort of enlightenment.

'Shit!' I said. Nothing; I couldn't make any connection. I was still fucking lost. I felt annoyed. I thought about it again; nothing. I had to take my mind out of that. I went to my desk and switched on my laptop and opened my word file on my desktop. I looked at the title of my romance novel *Morse* and I said, 'Fuck! Great! Just what I needed now! More fucking enigmas!' I couldn't take it anymore. I decided I need to go out and jog again. I couldn't think. I needed to relax my fucking head. I went out.

Marco Dias

CHAPTER 10

News from Earth

Nearly two weeks went by since I had my dream. I don't remember any more dreams since that day. In the meantime, I decided to put the photo frame and the wooden slate inside my drawer. I couldn't focus and I couldn't reach any conclusion, so I thought it would be better to hide them from me. Whatever that meant; whatever message was there for me, I felt that it would eventually find me again when necessary; I don't know. I tried to carry on my normal life and kept engaged with my romance novel trying to take my mind away from the last events. Maybe everything was in the end just a dream. But it wasn't. Something had changed inside my soul since my last trance. I don't know why, but I started praying again every night. I did not feel that it was because I believed in the words I mumbled in dark of the night before I went to sleep, but it was definitely calming me down. Slowly I could feel that my thoughts were getting more balanced. I slept like a baby after praying. Not quite sure what is the real connection by praying to your chosen God but no doubt that in a very mystical way it brings down our anxiety levels. In my novel I was halfway; the drama and I had reached a sensitive moment. You know you choose a happy ending for a story? Sometimes that choice is made before you start writing a story and then you just keep to it until the end; the plot comes to you and you accept it and you are happy with it and that's it. But very often a novel turns out to be just like itself or to make it clearer, like a marriage. When we fall in love and decide to get married, everything seems perfect and the world is a fairy tale, right? The reality, as many of us know, is that relationships are very fragile, and easily a great marriage turns into a fucking nightmare and just like that, everything that seemed destined to be forever quickly ceases to exist. That's how I felt in that moment with my novel; somehow, I knew that the end was another one. I stopped writing for a little while and went to the kitchen to make myself a coffee and have a cigarette outside in the rear patio. It was a fresh early spring morning. I had been writing non-stop since 7:00 in the morning and it was now 11:00; like in any another profession I had my rota well planned and I felt happy with it knowing that I was in the right way. Now it was my break; one hour or two, depending on my mood. I was relaxed sitting in my chair outside seeing planes flying low (many people were despairing with the sound that the airplanes did now by flying lower but I got used to it and it didn't bother me at all) with the shy sun hitting my body when an alert sound from my *New York Times* app popped out of my phone followed by another one. The first was about a few women, including the one from *Tomb Raider*, being victims of sexual abuse by a fellow called Harvey Weinstein. Maybe it was just another one of his productions, who knows? The second alert was about the G10 secret meeting taking in an unknown place on the 20th or the 21st of March just before spring. Today it was the 20th, so it could very well be that today the leaders of the free world would finally find a solution for the natural event happening on Earth denominated by the Death Line. Unfortunately for all humans, except you, my dear readers, none of them will be able to access this information. And I should advise not to share it with anyone else because you never what might happen. Remember what happens to those that don't know how to keep things under the hat and just talk too much? Exactly! In the end no one believes them, and they go from intelligent and respectful people to jerks, idiots and targets for elimination. Like I said and I repeat, this is confidential information, I laid my hands on because I am Portuguese and have a very good friend of mine working in one of the best seafood restaurants in Praia Dona Ana, Lagos, Algarve in the south of that beautiful country called Portugal. He worked at the 'Shark' (he managed to swipe in a mobile phone and send me this information before he died bleeding to death due to a clean, deep and surgical cut in his throat). It's António Guterres's favourite sea food restaurant. The restaurant was built in an isolated area on the edge of a rocky cliff overseeing a beach with beautiful thin white sand and bathed with calm tropical clear green and blue waters. It's a one-level building with an area of around 300 hundred squares metres with a 15 metres wide façade with thick glass instead of brick walls. A couple of sliding doors give way to a very nice woody terrace with more garden-style wooden tables surrounded by a stainless-steel structure of about 1.5 metres tall and with thick-cut glass as well. A fat and dense green bush wall gives one hundred per cent privacy against any unwelcome tourist passing by. It's one of those idyllic places, no doubt; relaxing and inspiring; just what those men needed to help us all. The restaurant had also a secret underground passage to a close-by villa with plenty of rooms and leisure areas for all of them to rest during the

parties (I meant between the meals and the agenda). Guterres had it all reserved for five days just in case the summit had to be extended and there was no white smoke lift-
ing from the chimney in the first two days. It was also
agreed that every gentleman was allowed to bring two of
their finest elite detail personnel just in case some information about this reunion had somehow been leaked to the
mass media and any people would use some common sense
and attempt a terrorist attack. I do apologise; I meant infi-
dels. Guterres called the previous day just to make sure
everything was on and promised paying in advance a million euros for the three days, which included obviously
paying for the food and beverage and chefs (plus a pastry
chef from Belem), porters and so on. I think that 50,000
euros was enough, but António was such a nice guy –come
on, the secretary for the United Nations – and he is all
about helping people; that and the fact that tax and donation
money was there just at hand. Why not?

'How much?' asked Guterres after the manager of
the restaurant told him over the phone with a not very confident voice. He had done his maths and 25,000 was more
than enough but why not risk 50, right? '50,000? Oh, come
on, my dear Judas! How long have we known each other?
How often do I go in there? Hey? How many times did you

offer dinner or lunch for free? Judas! I'm giving you one million euros! Ahaha! You just make sure everything is the way I like it and that you gather all the personnel in the end so we can thank you! How does this sound to you? I'll give you the cash then and if things are divine, I will add another bonus.'

Judas was exhilarated. He couldn't hold so much happiness inside him and he ended up letting go: 'Oh my Lord! Oh Jesus! Thank you, thank you, and thank you! Alleluia!

'There's no need to thank me, my dear friend! It's a pleasure!' And António finalised by saying, 'In the end before we leave, I'll give your pay, or would you rather get it now?'

'Oh no, sir, by all means, in the end it's fine.' The man was so happy! 'So, what time should I expect you, sir?'

'We will arrive there the latest at 10:00, so if we could have a few cocktails and nibbles for that time that would be perfect.'

'Of course, sir! Everything will be immaculately ready for you and your friends!' he answered in confident military tone. And that was it. Following their plan all of them arrived there at 10:00 on a minibus disguised as normal Chinese tourists so they wouldn't catch anyone's attention. The Japanese Prime Minister won the first prize for the best lookalike face and custom and of course Trump, because being American is being different, showed up, very surprisingly, dressed up as a Mexican with a lovely sombrero hat and a waxed black moustache. The detail personnel, because they came in pairs, dressed up in rainbow and pink motifs making them true fairies from the south; a heavy duty invisible drone dropped down a few wooden crates with guns and more relaxed wear for all of them at the restaurant's terrace; perfect plan. What else could be expected from people with so much imagination and influence like the members of the G10? – Excellence, nothing less. The big day had come. Oh my God! Everyone was so happy. Do you remember how you felt when you went on your spring break? That feeling of excitement and freedom! It's amazing, is it not? You, away from your parents in some distant exotic place with nothing else on your mind apart from getting drunk and having sex; how cool is that? That was exactly the feelings expressed in everyone's looks at that moment outside that restaurant on that sunny terrace in the Algarve. There was no wind. The temperature was already around 25 degrees and two tidy and sparklingly dressed waiters were standing by two tables covered with immaculate white cotton cloths with several of bottles of prosecco and champagne on it. The most radiant crystal flutes dispersed beautiful prism Newtonian colours in all directions under the light of the sun. What an image! Judas did know how to put on a show. Half a dozen large round tables, again with virgin cloths, were beautifully decorated equally with quartz jars with asters, white and red calla lilies inside and some daturas, dark violet-maroon orchids and hibiscus; I wonder why and who advised Judas to use these combinations of flowers? Maybe he had a dream about it or maybe he is getting emails from his pal Jesus in Heaven or perhaps these were the cheapest he could find, and as a good Jew he was just being natural and true to his commandments; monopoly of minds and monopoly of coins. Who knows? Everything is possible in the realm of imagination, right? Going back to the tables before we get in touch with the characters, I need to say that I love plat-ters with wild giant prawns and lobsters decorated with fresh lettuce and slices of lemon. There are, I'm sure, many symbolisms for the colour orange and red but I'm sure that joy and desire are two of them. The menu had been entrus-ted to Judas and he knew very well Guterres's tastes, so, apologising in advance to all members of the G10 and their detail personnel, but the menu would be based on his preferences and no one else's; but let's be fair, the Portuguese cuisine rivals with any of the best in the world and when it comes to seafood or fish we can be impressed – thou shalt not forget we conquered half of the world using boats. Equally divided in every table there were also platters with the finest prosciuttos, hams, cheeses and jams with many different flavours. From the kitchen the smell of the main courses was now invading the outside. In God's and the Devil's name, everyone was so happy they decided to start the party straight away without even bothering changing to more relaxed clothes. So there we have the most influential people on this planet celebrating an early spring break dressed up as Chinese and one Mexican; brilliant. But do not worry, they will find a way to make the majority happy; they always do. The shit chat was about to start. António Guterres would have the first word as he was the host of that amazing place; he raised his voice just for a moment and started: 'My friends, my friends! Please, let's gather here by the table. Please, just a quick one before we bring the house down. Please bring your glasses. I would like to make a toast, please join me here at the table.' And they all did with an honest smile on their face. He carried on: 'Thank you, thank you,' he kept saying until they were all together at the centre table whilst the detail personnel was busy checking every corner of the property and defending the perimeter; you know how it works; strategic defence locations and a few explosives here and there just in case someone managed to breach inside. Well, one thing they could give thanks to God and the Devil for was the Death Line; at least no big threat could come from above. Guterres carried on with a very confident and colloquial voice as if he was talking to all countries at the United Nations HQ: 'Thank you, thank you and thank you all for being here today with me in this amazing place. Thank you. I would like to add that I've hired the best personnel to take care of all of us...' and he looked towards Putin, 'the best pastry chef from Lisbon is here with us preparing specially for you our famous Belem custard pastries.' And he put a big smile on Putin's face who tilted his head up and down in approval and thought at the same time: that's very good news, your fat fuck; you just save me a couple of missiles. Guterres carried on: 'Moreover, I took the liberty of reserving the best food, beverage and accommodation for next five days, just in case we can't reach a solution by then and not to worry, we can stay much longer if you all wish it. There's something I would like to ask you all if there's no one against it; if you could just relieve yourselves of mobile phones or any other means of communication with the outside; I strongly believe that we need to focus here on helping God and our fellow earthlings, and so if you don't mind, one of my collaborators will pass now to collect it all.' And he called someone with his hand that showed up with a black leather suitcase where everyone dropped their devices. 'Please, no worry, all electronic equipment we need to use is now being installed in the conference room where we will head later in the afternoon after lunch. Thank you again for understanding. So, now let's all do a toast and start eating and drinking, my friends, inside they are already preparing everything for lunch. The world needs us!' he said as if he truly believed in it. They followed by raising their champagne flutes and cheered in unison: 'Early spring break!' Now it was time for more shit chat and naturally some subjects were more in vogue than others. So, let's say, Trump's big wall border against the Mexican threat and Brexit against the rest of the world were much more important than assistance for Africa, Ageing, AIDS, Atomic Energy, Children and so on – naturally. Actually, the big wall was what everyone really wanted to talk about because open markets and map borders were things of the past and if we look at geography, it makes a lot of sense building walls separating countries. The Chinese did it, the Germans did it and why don't the English do it with the Scottish, the Canadians with the Americans, the Japanese with Koreans and Russians, the Russians with eastern Europe, China, Mongolia and Kazakhstan and so on, why not? Let's all build walls, huh? It's definitely a good idea. Unsurprisingly, due to the extent of their borders, Putin and Trudeau were the two most interested in listening to what Trump had to say about it. Merkel was by now following Trudeau everywhere. I think she was starting to envision them all dressed with black leather tight wear. Who knows right?

Putin popped the question: 'My dear friend Trump, I think that your idea is one of the best in the history of mankind. I'm considering doing something like that. There's, however, something that I would like to ask you about it?' Putin made a small pause. He didn't want to look poor in Trump's eyes. He thought for a second and said: 'You know well that my country is, like yours, one of the richest and most powerful in the world, but I've invested recently a good amount of my people's money in nuclear research, and as you well know I lost of lot of money with space investigation as well... it will not be a problem, of course, but you are definitely the most successful businessman I know...'

'For God's sake! Just go straight to the point, you cocksucker! What do you want to know?' Trump interjected effusively, making Putin uncomfortable whilst everyone drafted a shy smile about this conversation. Trudeau decided to help Putin by, on the other hand, pushing Merkel away from his ass. She was by now getting a bit drunk and was spreading her wings over the handsome boy.

'What our friend wants to know, I believe, is how will you pay for the construction of your wall? Is it not, my dear friend?'

Putin nodded affirmatively. 'Ahaha.'

Trump loves the attention. He would be a showman if he didn't. 'OK, OK. I'll let you know how I will do it. It's very simple.' Everyone was now sitting down around one of the round tables eating prawns, lobster with their hands. Let's say that by now everyone was starting to get in touch with their true feelings. Blessed be the vines. T. had his show back. Everyone was waiting for him: 'UNESCO, casinos, prisoners and tourism!' T. declared triumphant; he carried on in a very confident manner: 'My friends, what's the point of spending money helping and developing poorer countries? Allowing them to become our competitors one day? Don't think so. Do as I tell you, get out of UNESCO. Casinos, my friends! That's definitely one of easiest ways of making money. Let's addict people and suck their bones! Don't forget that the edge is always on the house, right? Prisoners! All we need to do here is support criminality and then use the manpower of prisoners in the construction of the wall. Like the Chinese are doing in Africa and in other continents supporting their companies with high quality man work for an equal cost of slavery! And staying with the Chinese, those clever small red bastards, tourism! How many people in the world have visited the Great Wall of China? My friends, not only will my wall be easy and cheap to build but it will also in the near future bring me amazing profits! Ahaha! Ahaha!' Wow! Everyone was overwhelmed with Trump's plans. He is no doubt a clever bastard.

'A big applause for this man,' added Theresa May starting to her maths. 'Well, I have Brexit; maybe we can allow a few more million immigrants inside and then arrest them for trespassing; I mean, I have plenty of casinos; tourism is not an issue as well...' Everything was taking shape in her head. 'Bravo!' she shouted a bit unexpectedly. Inside the restaurant, lunch was nearly prepared. Waiters were just finalising the last touches under the supervision of a few of the detail personnel that by now had changed to their black suits; too manly to wear rainbow colours. Outside the

Chinese and the Mexican were marinating their blood with sparkling wines; more reds and whites were waiting inside and bourbons and whiskies and vodkas and other spirits. Everything was going according the plan. After lunch all of them would then be at their best to save the world. Don't worry; everything is going to be fine. Let's leave this bunch for a while and allow M. more time to understand his role in this story and let's go straight to Heaven where Mary and Cruz were about to reach God's lunch and then make the relations between M. and António hoping to find a proper solution for all this fucking mess.

Marco Dias

CHAPTER 11

The book of numbers and other revelations

'Oh, for fuck's sake! What the fuck is going on there?' This was Mary's reaction when she got the first glimpse of what was going on at her husband's lunch about 300 feet away from it.

'Calm down, my lady, please, I beg of you, please calm down.' Father Cruz was trying to help but he should have known better by now that the last thing you can say to someone who is upset is to calm down.

'Calm down! Calm down! What the fuck do you mean, calm down? Can't you see what the fuck is happening over there! Huh? Is this fucking Heaven or fucking Hell?' Cruz had just realised that he had added more wood into the fire and he decided to stay quiet shrugging his head in his shoulders like a turtle would do in the presence of danger.

'Ah!' Mary was fuming like a dragon. 'And what is this fucking smell!' she shouted. 'Is this pot I smell? Ah! I would kill him so bad if he could die!' Yes, it was pot, the highest quality. Everyone was drunk and high. God, the Devil, saints, demons, monkeys, zebras, even the birds above were stoned, having a laugh and holding hands. At this point and for the purpose of this story it's irrelevant to describe the fool expressions and philosophical conversations of all of them; for those that already got high, you know well what I mean and for those that haven't, I can only say by experience that you will not lose anything because in the end it's all a temporary illusion, a waste of time, money and many times the end of good friendships but nothing like hitting our heads a few times until we understand it. So, by all means if you want to try drugs, go and do it; it will be your problem, not mine anymore. In that moment, at that memorable lunch everyone was friends; everything was fine; there were no worries in the below or above the Death Line; yippie! What I'm going to say next should not be seen as binding, but it seems right very often; the advanced age of Father Cruz gave him a more sensible and wise vision of the world. Where Mary found only hate and despair the saint found an opportunity. The Virgin was blinded by rage. In a blink she saw herself beating everyone out of there with a broom on a moving fast forward speed movie picture. She was ready to kick some asses. Her eyeballs were popping out and her face was scarlet like a comic character. 'Grrrr!'

At this moment Father Cruz grabbed her by an arm and said with a very perceptive look: 'Wait, my lady! This is just what we need. Let's call it karma if you will.'

'Karma, karma? What the fuck do you mean?' Mary couldn't think straight. How could she? Her husband and her son high and drunk hanging out with the scum of the universe and giving lascivious looks to both monkey and zebra females; ewww, yuck; put rotten on that. 'Karma! I'll show what karma is!'

'No, no, no, Maria, please listen to me, I beg of you, please. I understand your anger but hear me; listen, listen, listen.' Mary was literally dragging him with her as she got closer and closer to where all of them were jamming. Cruz had to use a special word so he could attract her attention at that moment; only this word would freeze her: 'Revenge, revenge, Mary!' It was no doubt the best Christian thing to say and it worked to perfection. Mary stopped immediately and her features brightened from night to day.

'Vengeance, what do you mean, Father?'

Cruz took a few moments to get his breath back. 'Well, my lady, revenge or vengeance may not be the right words; what I meant was my book of numbers, remember?'

'What about your book of numbers?' Mary had calmed down, but she was still a bit upset with that sight just a few metres in front of her. 'Oh, the book of numbers, what about it?' It would take a while until she managed to focus. I believe that what she needed in this moment was jogging. It usually works for M. and for many others, maybe it would work for her.

'Your husband's and the Devil's crazy plan to avoid the end of the world? The Death Line? M. and A, remember, we were just talking about it a few moments ago, my lady?'

Mary fixed her attention on Cruz and finally managed to calm down. 'Oh, of course I remember, but how can this miserable scenery be of any use for us, Father?'

Father Cruz smiled and added: 'Well, my lady, for how long do you think this party will last and better than that, for how long do you think your husband will be with a hangover and—'

And Mary interrupted him: 'Oh, I know where you are going with this; alcohol and drugs work in Him like kryptonite for that Superman...You are very clever,

Father…we can use all this time to check the book of numbers and plan what to do without any concerns…he cannot Omni anything…Ahaha…'

'Exactly, my lady,' said Cruz, laughing. 'I think that the best thing to do is to avoid being seen because I'm sure no one remembers that we have left,' declared F.C. as he led Mary to another path leading to his monastery less than half a mile from God's villa. The way in and out from Africa was just a door away. Apart from God and the Devil everyone else used doors to change sets. All they need to do is to touch the door with their right hand and command it the desired destination and there you go. It works pretty much the same way in Hell with a small difference; they use the left. If you think about it, time and space travel isn't that complicated, is it? We have all seen it in many movies or read theories about it. It may sound stupid that people travel dimensions in Heaven by touching doors, but how stupid did someone look 1,000 years ago something different from having the Earth as the centre of the universe? In the end everything is wrong and everything is right at the same time because the real true question for knowledge will never be about being accurate or erroneous but about belief; we are and see who or what we choose to be or project in our minds. Maybe the Earth is the centre of the universe, maybe it's not; who can prove it or reject it? In conclusion, perhaps we are the only gods and demons, the true creators of heavens and hells. We are the vehicle of the silent vacuum. With this in mind, Cruz touched a few doors until he reached the quietude of his chambers; simple room with a simple single bed against a wall; small desk with a chair with a window in front of it overviewing the river Tejo. He got in with Mary and grabbed his book from his humble desk and they both went out to the mail hall that looked more like a library; it was a room without windows, with ceiling-tall bookshelves with books of numbers. It had a few leather sofas with small marble centre tables where the saints spent their days answering prayers and studying the numbers of Christianity. It's well known that society doesn't create saints so easily today as it did in the good old dark days; this is not because there aren't many around us; it's for the reason that people stopped believing in that and this is why saints up there research their books; to find more saints. The show   must go on.

Mary sat down at one of the tables whilst Cruz went to get the biblical numerology book from one of the shelves. Cruz sat down with her giving her a pencil and papyri sheet from his private reserve and said: 'Very well, shall we start, my lady?'

'Yes, Father, let's find a solution for what those two drunk bastards will create for our fellow humans in the near future... Ah, it will give so much pleasure throwing at their faces the right way to sort this shit; crappy Gods they will be in that moment; please, Father let's show them...' Mary was talking and searching in her future the images that would finally give her the spotlight she longed for. Her desire was no longer the end of the humans or the human race on Earth but embarrassing Gods. Cruz knew what was going in her mind; he saw how much she had suffered at His hands; he discerned what she wanted – revenge!

'Everything at its own due time, my dear Mary.' Cruz couldn't create feelings like hers in his mind but he was undoubtedly well acquainted with all of them; over and over again humans pray in his name and share their worst in search of absolution, it's that easy to be a Christian; no problem in sinning as long as you repent; a few Holy Fathers and another bunch of Hail Marys will put you on the right path again.

'Very well, Father, let's see what we have here,' declared the Virgin as a student being given the assignment of a lifetime.

'Yes, if you could please make note of their baptism numbers; M: PT/08/03/1976/08:00; and for António...give me one second; here we are: PT/05/04/1950/zero eight hundred hours…did you get it all?' he asked after telling Mary this numbers.

'Yes, Father, I wrote it down in flawlessness.'

'Perfect! Let's then start making the connections.' And as soon as he said this, they both looked at each other with a very concerned look.

'In my husband's name and in the name of the best, can this be true, Father Cruz? − 8 + 5 = 13, Father…we don't need this book anymore.' Cruz was caught by surprise. He told her the numbers and didn't even realise what he had just said: 8, 5, 13; many other relatives can be associated with these numbers but resurrection, grace upon grace and the Devil were the first popping into their minds.

Mary was suddenly frightened. 'For fuck's sake, Father! What does this mean? Is this somehow the work of my husband? I don't think we should pursue this option; maybe your dream was wrong, Cruz. I need to get out of here, Father.' Mary was uncomfortable. That room was shrinking in front of her judgments. She was seeing eyes and observing from the walls. Cruz was also a bit incredulous, but he knew better that everything happens for a reason. The reason he had become a saint wasn't due to God's destiny; the reason was because he was a true humanitarian; he believed and loved people. He did practise good in the name of men, not in the name of dubious writings written by partial people. Cruz would figure this out with the help of Mary. Mary is in the end a simple woman and as such one of the most sensible and edgy beings ever seen in the universe. They are, however, also the most intelligent and pragmatic. Father Cruz needed her help. He had to find a way to calm her down or to move her attention to a different topic, but how? Only he knows why but he said:

'Gabriel.' And it worked instantly.

'Gabriel, what do you mean?' she answered flushing at the same time.

'What, pardon?' replied Cruz, a bit lost and embarrassed at the same time and like I said, no one knows why he would say such a thing. 'Gabriel? Huh, no, I never said that. What I was saying was, maybe Hell…'

'Oh! What? Maybe Hell what?' Oops, awkward moment, but it worked. Mary was back on track. 'What are you saying, Father? How can Hell be of any use for us?

'Well, I'm not quite sure and I will need your help with this one.'

'OK, fair enough. I'm afraid I am a bit lost in here now,' answered the Virgin looking at the numbers she had written on her sheet. 'Please tell me what you are thinking, Father.'

He carried on telling her his thoughts while reading more information about the two subjects in his book. 'Very well, according to my book…can this be right?'

'What, Father, for fuck's sake, what's going on?' Mary was as impatient as any normal woman at this moment.

'Mary, António will die on March the 13th 2015…' Mary looked at him the same way a donkey looks at a Ferrari; is this food? This was starting to feel a bit out of her league.

'Wait a second, Father, please; I'm getting lost in here. If he is going to die in 2015, how is that any good for us now? The apocalypse is next year; what are you not telling me, Cruz? There's more to this than just your dream, is there not?' There was a moment of silence and before Cruz could say something Mary made use of a few common denominators; intelligence and pragmatics. 'Can I ask you something, Father?' He nodded affirmatively. 'How true is "determining your destiny" 49:1-28 in my son's book, Father? My husband's Book of Destiny was never stolen by the Devil, was it? Cruz, are you the one hiding the book?' I need now, as the storyteller to pause this moment, when Mary and Cruz are sitting in the saint's library trying to find a solution for the future because I feel that you, my dear readers, may feel a bit lost too. That being so, you understand what these two are talking about; I must tell you about a very old legend. There is a myth in Heaven about a Book of Destiny. Rumours say that in the beginning of all things, before the universe and our Earth and men were given free will, God in his omnipotence sat down one day and wrote down the Book of Destiny. God is selfish but in those days he was also a bully, and as such he thought that it would be better to create a race he could control easily; and what better way to do it than allow humans the idea of pursuing their dreams? Of course, in the end our dreams were nothing more than illusions. According to the same stories God got more interested in us as time went by through the millennia and he felt bored with his book. Let's say that if someone tells us how a book or a movie is going to end, it's not interesting anymore. Naturally, being God and having these thoughts in his mind, regret is not enough because humans would still be a projection of his deepest desires. It is said that it was because of this that Jesus came to Earth, so we could somehow choose our own destiny. Now the question is, would you destroy a medal that you own; would you let go of something or someone who was dear? It is said that God can do everything he wants and maybe the same way he created our destiny, perhaps he clicked a finger and undid it all. I have my doubts. How often is science left out with answers for so many things happening here? Why are so many of us so caring, honest and hardworking and spend our lives miserably; and how many of us are exactly the opposite when we triumph like kings? I think that God never managed to clear his mind of all the thoughts he wrote down in his book, making us half-true and half-free willed, but that's just my opinion. Now let's go back to Heaven and read what Father Cruz has to say about this story: '… are you hiding this book?'

Cruz knew he couldn't omit this anymore. He took a moment breathing profoundly, searching his memories into the exact moment he acquired the Book of Destiny; he said finally as he slowly got up from his chair, 'Please follow me, my lady, there's something I need to show you,' and he moved towards a big shelving unit where he touched a few books as if he was inputting a secret code in a digital screen; when he touched the last book *The Origin of the Species* by C.D. a click was heard on the opposite side of the library and another book slid slowly outside; it was the Huxley-Wilberforce debate. He then opened that book on page 13, line 7 and read: '…either it has always been here, or it had beginning'... A few seconds of silence and the sound of pulleys was heard for about 20 seconds and finally one last book slid out opening a door unveiling behind it a small room all covered in silver aluminium and in the centre of this room there was a wooden lectern with another book on it. The last book to slide was a book by Georges Lemaitre, on the top of the podium a hallowed Old Testament was resting; Cruz led a very disbelieving Virgin Mary inside and closed the door behind them; still holding her hand he laid his other hand on the top of the Old Testament and mumbled a few indistinct words; then he stepped back and waited in silence. Slowly and magically the front hard cover folded unveiling inside a slightly smaller book; it was a black hard cover book with this title imprinted in gold: '01010100 01101000 01100101 00100000 01100010 01101111 01101111 01101011 00100000 01101111 01100110 00100000 01100100 01100101 01110011 01110100 01101001 01101110 01111001' – the Book of Destiny.

CHAPTER 12

Ascending

'I need to relax my fucking head! Why is this shit happening to me?' It was late afternoon when I wake up from another dream – or I'll better call it nightmare – I don't know what to think anymore. 'I have had enough of this shit! Leave me alone!' – I didn't even know who I was asking to leave me alone. You know when it looks as if everything in your life turns into a rollercoaster of successive unexpected events; sometimes good, sometimes bad? Let's say you start by waking up early morning having had an awful and short night of sleep; you wake up in a bad mood and your car doesn't want to start for some unknown reason; and then you get a call from your ex asking for more money for an unexpected extra bill because your child has broken his glasses in a stupid fight at school and then you get a call from your best friend asking for more money because he had some trouble in his life; then you get an alert message from your credit card provider telling that your statement is red; then when you get to work, one or two of your members of staff decided to call in sick; and maybe you will even get a message from your child asking if he can spend a pound online to buy a pack a diamonds so he can extend his dinosaurs' island? You know what I mean, don't you? That's exactly how I was feeling in that moment when I left my house in Brighton and headed towards the waterfront by the marina. If I was asked to write a poem at that moment, I would have to call it 'Fucking hell'. It was 6:30pm and it was a lovely sunny afternoon and apart from a fisherman sitting very close to where I usually sit, the beach was deserted. I thought about jogging. I decided to go and sit down in silence close to the fisherman. I was annoyed and helping things getting even better I had forgotten my wallet, my cigarettes and my phone at home. Fucking great! And I desperately needed a damned cigarette. I looked at the fisherman for a few minutes and nothing; no cigarettes and no fish. Fucking useless you are! I thought. I fixed my vision near the horizon line around eight miles away into the English Channel or La Manche for the French and started counting turbines to the left and to the right of one of the platforms of the Rampion Wind Farm. The evening mist was blurring my viewing and I was getting lost all the time; fuck this shit! I stopped counting. The twilight was closing by. The temperature would drop down ten degrees in a blink. I looked at the fisherman again and he looked at me. I don't know what he was thinking, but he was maddening me. I grabbed a couple of rocks and started playing with them in my hands and kept watching him while he prepared to cast another try into the sea. He looked at me, opened the bait with one hand and targeted his rod at a specific point in the water, maybe 50 metres ahead just in front of where I was sitting and sat down, still looking at me. 'What the fuck do you want?' I mumbled, getting angry. I gave him a defying look, got up and threw a rock exactly to where his cast had fallen. He got up instantly and gestured at me from the near distance. I did same and shouted at him: 'What, do you fucking own the sea now?' I had a crazy look in my eyes. I felt that he wanted to say something, but he didn't and sat down again, tilting his head right and left showing some sort of pity for me. What the fuck am I doing? What's wrong with me? I need a cigarette. I fucking need a cigarette! I should have apologised for my attitude, but I didn't. I could feel my blood boiling. I decide to abandon the beach and head home. I needed a cigarette and I needed to get drunk and I needed drugs. My plan was simple; get home, change and go out to the city and get wasted. No one, no jogging and no writing would help in that moment. I wanted to forget; I wanted to become hallowed and so I did. I wasn't myself in that instant. I felt as if some other entity was trying to take over my reasoning. Maybe I was just being absorbed by the general energy on Earth. Perhaps it was just another bad dream, but it wasn't. I always saw myself as a good man and I have many friends who can testify that what I'm saying is true. Often people come to me for advice for their life and they genuinely feel better when they are around me. I've always thought about myself as a magnet of good, but something was changing in my mind and in my heart. Where is the good old funny M.? I could feel the good in me slipping away from the tip of my fingers, but why was this happening to me? Why was I given those stupid wooden artefacts? Who had plans for me, and where the fuck was I going to fit in it? Why did I not just sit down in front of my computer that night and vomit away everything that was mutating me inside? Why did I go out that night? Why, even knowing what is right or wrong, do we most of the times choose the wrong path? Why are we given free will and our life feels predestined? Was mankind's fate already written in some absurd and selfish book? I honestly don't know. M.

had always been a troubled human being, but he is no different from any of you; all of us are demi-gods because in all of us there's an angel and demon waiting to come out. Sometimes we freely choose our future, other times the world we live in chooses on our behalf and occasionally the skies above decide our fate. M. was suddenly angry at the world. He got home infuriated for no reason other than feeling lost and how feeling like that can change us and the world around us. How often depression leads to suicide and how can you explain war if not for the same reason? Depression clouds our reasoning, it's a fact, but that will be the subject of another fiction maybe called 'Maria'. He got home, opened the door and slammed it behind him. What he needed was a cigarette, but he had forgotten about it. What the fuck is wrong with me! Focus, I kept telling myself; focus on something good; the image of your son; the image of my mother; the image of a paradisiac island; a sunny day; my father! No, not my father! I can't think of him now! Why did you take my father from me, you fucking asshole! I looked up x-raying the ceiling of my room trying to see God through it. Why did you take my father from me in his sleep, why, you selfish piece of shit? I kept talking to myself looking for my wasted blue skinny jeans and my cherry Doc Marten boots. You don't even fucking exist, do you, you prick? My blood was boiling in anger. I sat down on my bed and picked my red weekend offender t-shirt looking at the brown carpet just there two feet away from me. I couldn't think straight, my head was blowing; what the fuck is going on with me? I looked at my chest of drawers and on top of it I could see the two wooden artefacts; maybe I left there when I left a while ago, maybe I forgot to put them inside the drawer, thought I. The more I looked at it the further my anger grew. What the fuck do you mean and why the fuck was it given to me? My room started shrinking on me. I started panicking. I felt like my blood pressure went up to 240 over 140. I needed to calm down or hit something or someone, perhaps…no, no, what the fuck am I thinking about? I got up infuriated and grabbed my wallet and my keys from the top of the drawer and slapped harshly the slate and the wooden frame against the wall, causing them to fall over my bed and an 'I' shape scratched on the white wall. As I left the room moving to the kitchen I saw the picture of my son pinned on my big notice board; I felt my body moving in slow motion as I left the room; his image was pulling me back, but something else equal to love dragged me out and quickly erased that image from my mind. My heart quickened to the speed of a bird's; I took a can of beer from the fridge, opened and drank it in one go; I followed by opening a bottle of red wine and had half of it non-stop. My heart was still quickening. I need more, I thought. I had the rest of the wine. I sat down and looked up at the kitchen cabinet where one of my mates had his stash of weed; I got up and quickly rolled a joint. I took another beer from the fridge and drank it at the same time as I smoked the spliff. – Whew. This shit is good. I had momentarily calmed down under the effect of the THC, but very soon the alcohol would start kicking in and then I change; euphoria. Yahoo! Fuck it, I'm ready, let's do this shit! I got up from the chair feeling calm and relaxed, and when I felt like I was coming back to reality, as I went out, my world slowed down again and my arm reached inside one of the kitchen drawers and my hand placed inside one of my back pocket jeans a thick and sharp metal fork. I don't know why my body acted like that and I went out without thinking about it anymore; it felt like I was entranced – you know when we drive a car from one point to another and we get there surprised without remembering doing it? The alcohol was by now navigating my blood at will. The dawn had just set in as I walked robotically towards the seafront near the marina, from where I would then follow the waterfront path along Madeira Drive leading to Brighton pier and the city centre. Fuck, I forgot my cigarettes again! It wasn't a problem this time; I had my wallet on me. I stopped at a convenience on Whitehawk Road and bought smokes, a lighter and another beer. Now I was ready. I crossed Marine Parade Road and stopped on the top wall overseeing the marina, the sea, the beach and the pier and Brighton's city centre lights about 1.5 miles away. I had a plan in my mind, a very simple plan; hit town, get wasted and wake up with a headache somewhere near the sea alone or in another place with female company. I went down to Madeira Drive but halfway there my body changed direction to a narrow path that leads the same way but that crosses a bushy garden where both male and female prostitution takes place. I respect it, but it disgusts me. I don't know why I went there but I did. It was dark and quiet. I walked slowly passing three or four wooden benches facing the sea. As I got closer to the bushy area, exactly on the last bench a small thin feminine figure dressed in black started to take shape. As I got close to her, she turned her face to me and strangely she wasn't afraid. I guess that the way I dress added to my short, faded haircut and my beard is common nowadays. She was a beautiful, brownish-skinned girl, surely 15 or 16 years old. I said Hi and she said Hi back to me. She looked me in the eyes; lovely dark brown eyes. It felt as if she was waiting for another question. She was holding a book in her hands. Something was definitely off in that scenario. Can I sit here with you? She nodded yes with her head. I could feel the school and the THC partying in my veins. I was euphoric inside but ghostly quiet on the outside. I stayed for a few seconds watching a few bright lights from fishing boats in the dark sea. Inside my tunnel vision I saw her turning a page very slowly. I glanced at her in slow motion and said with a cold but caring voice:

'Are you OK?' She said yes.

'Humm; can I ask you what you are doing here in this place alone?'

She promptly and confidently answered: 'I'm reading a book.'

'Humm; can you read with this light?' I asked, looking at the shy light coming from a nearby lamp.

'Yes.'

'I see…and do you like the book?'

'Yes.'

'OK. And what is your book about?' At that point I noticed that every time she answered my questions she would look at me first, but her eyes kept quickly glancing towards a narrow tarmac path disappearing into the bushes on my right-hand side. I divided my attention between her and the dark sea in front of me. I wanted to look at that path, but my body didn't want to. I could, however, even looking forward, distinguish the different dark colours in the place she moved to rapidly. I could identify a few different shades of green and one straight line of dark grey from the path narrowing in a V shape. Every now and then I could swear the stillness of those colours was disturbed by a different toned shadow. My body was straight and stiff, only my right arm and my hand started descending in very slow motion towards my back pocket; I don't know why.

'It's a fiction novel,' she said.

'I see. What about?' I asked, seeing again an indistinct shade moving at the end of the path. My hand reached closer to my pocket; again, my body was acting of its own free will.

'It's a fiction novel about the end of times,' she answered in very clear English but with a Latin accent.

'Oh, really, do you like that?'

'Yes, very much.' A longer moment of silence took place. Only the sound of engines going by on the road above, the squawking of a seagull now and then and the wind hitting the bushes made any sense at that moment.

I closed my eyes for a while and breathed profoundly before I said: 'So, everything is OK with you?'

'Hum hum.'

'And you are not afraid of being here by yourself?'

'No.' But this time there was a twist in her voice, I felt it; it struck me that she wasn't there willingly, but somehow, she felt safe. I got up the same I had sat, in slow motion. I looked at her and she looked at me. I couldn't see any emotion in her eyes. It was as if my concern was indifferent to her, but at the same time it was as if her eyes were crying for help.

I was standing up facing her when my hand reached my back pocket when I asked her one last thing: 'May I know your name?'

She slowly lifted her chin, closed her eyes and turned her head to the left, exposing her jugular and answered: 'Maria. My name is Maria da Cruz.'

'Maria. That's a beautiful name.' Following the last syllable of my last sentence '-me', my eyes shut down and I felt the whole world quake. My body turned the opposite way where her body stayed but my eyes only opened to reality a few feet away when I entered the narrow path between the bushes heading to Brighton pier 1.4 miles away. At the end of the path I could now distinguish another dark shape. I couldn't be positive if it was just a trick of my imagination or if it was a feminine or male silhouette. I wasn't afraid, I felt exactly the opposite of that, but it wasn't just confidence, it was something more powerful than that; a feeling that should belong only to non-humans, maybe gods, demi-gods, angels or demons. Whatever it was; a walk of good or bad faith, something or someone had control over my body and my soul. Perhaps my body was commanded by one entity and my trance by another. I moved slowly towards that dark outline, but I wasn't walking, I was gliding, or it felt like that. Once again as I got closer my arm and my hand moved to my back pocket without any thoughts. My body glided up to ten feet from that strange shape standing still in the middle of the footpath; it was another woman. I couldn't distinguish her features and she probably couldn't see mine. The light was very poor, coming only from a shy lamp standing 25 feet behind her.

'Who are you?' she asked in a calm, cold, metallic voice.

'I don't know who I am,' I answered sincerely as if I was confessing myself in a church; my hand moved inside my pocket at the same time as her hand grabbed an indistinct small dark object from her purse. It looked like a small gun. She pointed it at me.

'Who are you and why did you do what you did to my daughter? Why did you do that to her?' Her voice was giving many different feelings: anger, resignation, but mostly fear. I heard what she said, the way she said it, and somehow it all made sense   inside me.

'Why are you afraid of me?' I said before I spoke anything else and at the same time my body started moving towards her at a slug speed. She didn't answer and she stepped back once more, stretching her arm and pointing the object at me. I wasn't afraid. Whatever she had in her hand wasn't having any effect on me and my sliding did not stop. I spoke slowly, pausing a few seconds between the next things I told and asked her. 'I haven't done any-thing to her.' (Pause) 'I think that question you have to make is what have you done to her?' (Pause) 'Why was your child alone in the dark in that isolated place?' (Pause) I was dormant but I could feel my blood boiling inside. 'Is she your daughter?' (Pause) 'What sort of mother are you?' (Pause) 'Will you answer me?' (Pause) She never answered any of those questions. The whole picture shook again and went out of focus. My eyes shut down, but even with them closed I could see – not hear – half a dozen sparks shining on her hand. I don't think it had any effect on me at that otherwise I would not be here now.

'Who are you? Who are you? You are a ...' This was the only sound I heard fading away as my shadow mixed with hers for a dance I had never danced before. Again, I walked away without looking back. I was sure everything was fine behind me; exactly the way it should. The path elongated with a few twists between the bushes until it opened to the road not too far from the bar Concorde. I glided slowly in silence until I heard voices whispering in a hidden area of the vegetation. There was no clear man-made path to that place but time had made the bushes understand that they should not grow there. My plan had been to go to the town since I had left home but again my body stopped and turned to face that trail. The whispering stopped as he moved inside the scrubs. It didn't take me long to reach a small clearing where too male figures were sitting down on a park bench that surely someone had transported there. There a deadly moment of silence interrupted by the voice of one of them.

'Hey, cocksucker, what the fuck are you doing here, M.?' That voice struck familiar, but I couldn't yet tell who it was.

'Hey, mother fucker! What's going on, my friend?'
My hand distanced from my pocket. Those two voices brought me back to something close to reality; I

wasn't in charge of myself, however. They got up and came closer to me, giving me their hands to shake. I knew who they were now; it was J and J; two of my other housemates. They were smoking weed and offered it to me; I accepted it.

'What are you up to, mate?' asked J.

'Are you looking for company here in the bushes?' added the other J with a naughty laugh (they were both gay but they knew I was not).

'I'm not quite sure. I feel that I was heading to the city centre to a pub but I felt I should take this path and then something else pushed me to this place.'

They both laughed at me. 'No need to explain, mate, we know you are crazy; you are going to the city, where to?' asked one of the Js with another laugh. I handed him the joint.

'I'm not sure, I didn't really have any plans, I just needed to get out of my place and I don't even remember any more for what reason.'

They looked at each other and mumbled something I couldn't understand and then J said, 'You are fucked, man. I know what you need.' And he showed me a small bag with some bitter sugar crystals inside. 'Mandy! Mandy, that's what you need, man!' I nodded affirmatively, and he followed by splitting equally the amount he had in the bag for the three of us. He handed me the equivalent of an average pea. 'Eat that shit; you are going to be just fine!' said J, confident that he knew what I needed.

'Here, have a beer and sit down in there,' said the other J. I accepted the crystals and the beer, but I declared I was all right where I was standing (blocking the exit of that small space). 'It's all right. As you wish. Just have that shit!' They both sat down on the bench mumbling something again and laughing silently. They took their crystals and started drinking. One of them played a song on his phone. It was drum and bass. 'Take that shit, you cock!' I could see much of their faces again; I took the piece of crystal and chewed it like a gum. The most bitter taste I've ever had poisoned my mouth. I swallowed it all and washed it down with beer. I took less than a minute until the music's fast breakbeats invaded my body; my head started moving in the rhythm as the heavy bass. I started gritting my teeth. Something new was kicking in; the sound of the wind dancing with the trees, bushes, smaller plants, big and small leaves; I could hear it all; I could feel it all. My hand moved again slowly into my back pocket. New shades of dark and green were now brightening to a near daylight image. I was alone again. I thought I heard people laughing around me and my name being called several times: 'M., M., M., M., and M.?' I closed my eyes again and absorbed it all. I felt my hand touching warm metal. I breathed intensely and about a minute after my body turned back and started walking. I opened my eyes again once my feet touched the hard tarmac surface of the pathway. I was so strangely relaxed. I felt as if I didn't have a body anymore. I was now as the air embracing the forms of things. I wasn't human anymore. I had become energy. I was an atom. The way I felt had no reasoning for a word called molecule. For you to understand it better, I had travelled back in time to a place where D made more sense than DNA. I reached the main road facing the pier and it felt as if I had travelled to 1605 to the moment that Guy Fawkes successfully blew up the Houses of Parliament, but he didn't. I felt like transported to an amazing 5th of November bonfire. The lights had acquired an extraordinary glow and I felt Brighton calling me: 'Come to me!' And I went. Don't remember how I got there; I was just suddenly there. It was busy near the pier. I like it when it's busy. Somehow, I felt in charge of myself again. It was obviously a false control; I was now under Merck chemical domination or something like that, but it felt great. Ever since I left my house that night, I sensed I had been entranced by my own anger and despair. The ecstasy, together with THC and alcohol had given me back the confidence I had recently lost. I decided to head to the city centre and buy a bottle of rum at a convenience store in front of the Royal Pavilion Tavern, just after the RBS and then I made my way to the Royal Pavilion Gardens where I sat down under a tree. As usual the city centre was packed with drunk and drugged teenagers doing what they do best; have fun. When I was their age, I did the same and even now I'm doing it. As I walked there and maybe due to all the relaxed imagery, it hit me that not everything in the world is going that well. Flashes of planes vaporising in the sky invaded my imagination mixed together with the images of my wooden tokens. Again, I felt compelled to go to a specific point of that garden and I went. I sat down under a big tree at the eastern part of the park not too far from the north exit. The park was full of groups of young people doing their thing; same all, same all; drinking, taking drugs, chatting, laughing, screaming, dancing, running around like chickens and even some crying, fighting and some sex at will; youth at its best. If I was an actor, the place I was compelled to sit, would, no doubts, be the spotlight. A yellow lamp nearby gave me and that place a missed medieval renaissance glare. I sat down with my back straight against the tree and with my legs stretched and crossed. I opened the bottle of rum and lit a cigarette and drunk a quarter of the bottle in one go. I sensed many eyes looking at me in that place. I didn't care about it. My head started tilting up and down at the rhythm of Japanese trip hop. The shapes of the people nearby and the sounds they made slowly turned into a pleasant breeze. I drunk another third of the bottle and had another cigarette. My eyes found a familiar point in the distance and focused there. It was a big TV screen. There was a movie going on. I was seeing flashes of my past life; moments of my childhood; my father was in all of them. I smiled and hurt every time I see him. I feel my heart mutating in a flesh photo frame; on the right side there's a picture of a happy confident man fixing a broken tunnel carved in yellow sand; on the left side there's a picture of me crying, kissing his cold grey face inside a wooden coffin. People say that time heals everything, but that's a lie; time doesn't even exist. For those that were fortunate in having a loving and caring father like I had, you know what I am talking about. The pain will never go away. I was again entranced by something. The movie carried on displaying more images of good and bad moments in a quick fade in and out and between that fade I could see an alternate parade of both the slate and the wooden frame. My head kept tilting up and down with an imaginary beat. I finished the bottle and felt invigorated as if I had had a big glass of water. The giant screen had disappeared, and I was again surrounded by the crowds of Brighton; all of them were staring at me in silence and without faces. I wasn't afraid. I breathed deeply for a few seconds; I followed by taking my wallet from my pocket and threw it to the grass in front of me; it landed 20 feet away from me, halfway to everyone else; after I closed my eyes; my right hand reached my pocket again and my left hand placed itself over my heart; nothing. I kept breathing and nothing; either I was dead, or I didn't have a heart anymore. The voice of my father spoke in my mind:

M., M., M.?

It's time to leave M. alone in that park. Something took a back seat in his consciousness and personality; metamorphosis was about to take place. The reasons for what is about to happen and for what will come after might very well be found in Heaven but, before we go up to Heaven, let's go down to the Algarve in the south of Portugal. The magnificent ten are finishing their lunch and are about to move to another room. After the most succulent and refined courses of fish and cuts of meat, the finest desserts, spirits and liqueurs are waiting for the Gs in the conference lounge. It's time for sit down, relax and planning.

CHAPTER 13

White smoke

Old MacDonald had a farm,
E-I-E-I-O.

And on his farm he had some chicks,
E-I-E-I-O.

With a chick, chick here,
And a chick, chick there,
Here a chick, there a chick,
Everywhere a chick, chick,

Old MacDonald had a farm,
E-I-E-I-O.

2. Duck – quack
3. Turkey – gobble
4. Pig – oink, oink
5. Cow – moo, moo
6. Cat – meow, meow
7. Mule – heehaw
8. Dog – bow wow
9. Turtle – nerp, nerp

Needless to say, at this point this was the spirit in that res-taurant in the Algarve in the south of Portugal. The morn-ing Prosecco and the champagne were now mixed with the best reds and whites Portugal has to offer.

'*Mesdames et Messieurs, s'il vous plait.*' It was Guterres and the alcohol in his brains talking French, point-ing to a door at the back of the dinner where the conference lounge was waiting for them. Everybody was in such a great mood; laughs and smiles and taps on the back; what a wonderful world they live in. The truth must be said: Gu-terres does know how to throw a party. At this point one of the porters came in the main room and made a sign to the Gs letting them know that everything was ready inside the lounge that was situated just above that one.

'Come on, let's move, my little Japanese friend; the past is the past and let's be fair, you little crazy kamikazes were asking for a few bombs, were you not?' said Trump with an open smile whilst putting one arm around Shinzô Abe's back and leading him to the other room and to whom he answered with a yellow smirk, 'Me no Japanese, me Chinese.'

The German Chancellor was way over her head by now and she was trying a threesome with Trudeau and Mat-tarella. That's what it looked like seeing her going inside the lounge holding hands with both of them. I'm not quite sure, but it seemed that something was going on between Macron and May. There was definitely a certain degree of intimacy as they walked together to the other room. Maybe they were making friends like the American and the Japanese trying to put behind their backs the battle of Agincourt; who knows? Nothing like a good old piss-up to bring the best out of humans, don't you agree? Junker and Putin had a more reserved conversation going on, since before lunch, just after Trump had explained the benefits of a nice great wall for a nation. If I had to guess, I would say that Putin was still trying to convince the President of the European Union of the fairness of including a few more eastern countries under the Russian autonomy. Because they whispered all the time I can't be sure of what they were talking about, but it had to be, naturally, a monologue by Putin:

'I'm sure you agree with what I am proposing here because I'm a fair man, as you well know.' Certainly, after each statement, he would prove his points by adding something like: 'You know all those countries are Russian territory, and I can always drop a few bombs over Brussels to prove I'm right; don't you agree, my dear friend?' To whom Junker always delivered a sincere affirmative head, nodding. Guterres was the most excited one. He had to be.

Come on, how often in life do we manage to get our old buddies together for a good old spring break in a beautiful sunny country at a magic place by the sea? OMG, he was so happy! He reminded me of a shepherd dog running around, barking and playing; making sure the cattle goes safe inside the barn. For fuck's sake, God; give the man a tale so he can really express how happy he feels! G made sure everyone was inside and signalled one of his detailed guards to come and finish the job; the door was to be locked from the outside and under no circumstances were they to be bothered. They were men on a mission. It was a big room with a beautiful view over the sea. There was a nice wooden bar in the corner with the finest beverages you can think of and a proper espresso coffee machine; a huge central U shape grey sectional sofa area with capacity for 14 people altogether. It had a beautiful big glass table in its centre with an open box of cigars; two or three ashtrays spread equally on it and a musical metal triangle with what seemed to be a sheet with codes underneath it. There were also two closed small boxes with cocaine, cannabis and ecstasy in it, just in case there were any addicts taking care of the world; Guterres is an amazing host, is he not? Look at the detail he puts on everything. There were also ten small notebooks and ten pens with which they would create ideas to sort out the world. Against one wall there were three immaculately arranged tables with most tempting delicacies on it. There were two other doors; one accessed the toilets and the other one hid the secret passage to the rest area in a different building a few hundred metres away from the restaurant. A very old, well-trained deaf blind waiter was hired by Mattarella to take care of the needs of the magnificent ones. The security detail stayed outside protecting the Gs and making sure none of the employees of that restaurant would leave the premises and had a long healthy life in front of them. Everyone was amazed with the abilities of the waiter.

'For fuck's sake, is he really blind and deaf? I can't believe it! Can you fix me one of these?' whispered Trump, overwhelmed with that negro, naked from his waist up, standing still a few feet away from the centre sofas.

'No need to whisper, my friends. Observe: what would you like to have?' asked Mattarella, the owner of that specimen. Putin was the first to raise his hand and requested a glass of vodka and two Portuguese custards. Trump was about to put a request too when Mattarella said: 'No, please, let's do this one at the time so you can see good he is.' He then grabbed the musical triangle and the sheet of codes from the table and hit the metal several times in frequency similar to Morse code. 'Skin sonar interpretation. I've implanted a small metal bar in his brain,' said Mattarella proudly. And like that, for great amusement and amazement of the magnificent ten, the poor old negro went back and forward ten times until everyone's request was satisfied.

'Brilliant!' declared Guterres and he carried on with a more colloquial tone, 'My dear sirs, I hope you are enjoying this little venue I've arranged for us all and if you need something else, please let me know and I'll take care of it.' Everyone stayed in silence marinating the food and beverage inside their stomachs; good job, Guterres, I would say. 'I believe the time has come for all of us to start writing down ideas. It would be, I'm sure, in everyone's best interest to sort this out as quickly as we can. No doubt God has given us a hard task, but that just proves how much he respects and trusts our discernment.' Shinzô made a bored expression; Guterres carried on: 'On the table, as you can see, there's paper and pens for everyone, so I propose that individually, all of us come up with a few ideas and then together let's decide which are the best so we can e-mail them to God. I think one hour should be enough for that, and of course if you want something else to drink or bite, the triangle is on the table, just help yourselves.' Everyone nodded affirmatively, but Trump had something very important to say; he blinked at Putin and grabbed the metal triangle and sheet with codes and hit it around 51 times. The whole world waited for a few minutes until the waiter came with a tray with ten tall glasses with a dark brown drink inside.

Trump blinked his eye to Putin and raised his arm for cheers. 'Let's do this shit!' What drink do you think he ordered for all of them? I leave that one for your imagination. The game was on. For the next hour

with a laugh, laugh here,
And a laugh, laugh there,
Here a laugh, there a laugh,
Everywhere a laugh, laugh,

the Gs started writing their best ideas on their papers. They were happy. They felt like they were back in time to primary school, using a pen and paper for the first time, creating the most amazing stories. How wonderful for most of us, was it not? How beautiful it is being pure without knowing the wrongs in this world? Let's leave them with their thoughts for a few more minutes; let's leave God and the Devil at their party; Mary and Cruz inside their secret room and M.'s metamorphosis at the Royal Pavilion Gardens and take a minute to breathe and be honest with ourselves, shall we? Deep breath, please; please close your eyes and breathe profoundly a few times. Have you done it? Perfect. Now think with me; how did I come into this world? Who am I? What do I believe in? What makes me happy? What is my role in this world and in my happiness? What am I doing to be happy? Am I happy with the state of my world? Can I help making things better? Do I care? How many more questions? How many more excuses? For how long can we postpone the evil in people? Let me rephrase all these questions in one more understandable: what the fuck are we doing in this universe and why the fuck don't we care about anything? I want you to inhale sincerely again so we can go back to this story; deep exhale, please? Thank you. Back to Lounge. It was nearly teatime. Merkel was the first one to finish, laying down her sheet on the table followed by laying down one hand on Trudeau's leg and the other on Macron's whilst keeping an eye on the negro nearby; what a stupid smile she had stamped on her face. There's definitely an acute sense of pragmatics in the Germans; think smart, so they say. One after the other, all of them finished their task. It was time for tea break. This time Merkel grabbed the metal triangle and ordered ten *aromatiques* for everyone. By now the effect of the alcohol was starting to show on their faces; some were getting sleepy and the rest could barely stand with their backs straight against the sofa; not a problem; these were people on a mission and no doubt they would make smoke this afternoon. Not much was being said at this point. They were all very reflective. Trump and Mattarella were having a cigar and May and Guterres were rolling a king-size joint for everyone. Shinzô placed the cocaine on the table and was relaxing with it, with his pen, as if he had been given a small sand Zen garden. The drinks arrived silently delivered by two negros.

'Ahaha, there are two of them now!'

'Ahaha. You are damning right! How did this happen? Ahaha!'

The women were starting to lose it, but don't worry, everything is under control; we have the best people in the universe taking care of the Earth's interests, don't you agree? If you disagree, maybe next time you are given the opportunity to vote, maybe then you can take a stand. It's so easy to sit in front of a TV, or go out to a pub and complain about the state of things, isn't it? Well, stop fucking complaining and do something about it; just like these extraordinary people are doing now!

'Very well done, my friends! How is everyone feeling, all right? Good, perfect! Maybe we can have coffee now and eat something else, what do you think?' Guterres always the perfect host. All the others mumbled a few indistinct sentences, like: yeah, whatever and so on?

'Can I do it?' asked May without waiting for answer. She then followed by grabbing the metal triangle, hitting it randomly as if she was creating a song and making the old negro go around in circles completely out of tune. Everyone had a laugh and the lazy atmosphere was brought a few notches up with this clown act from the English Prime Minister.

'For fuck's sake, give me that shit,' intervened Shinzô with a serious face that melted into an uncontrollable laugh as he carried on playing another nonsense song with the triangle. At this point the negro stood his ground and stopped with a calm and relaxed attitude facing them near the bar. He was happy. He knew well that there are many people in this world that don't know how to interpret signs or symbols. He was OK with the life he had. He felt like the shepherd on the hills with his sheep; happy, simple people in a happy, simple world. There was a moment of silence, during the time the negro calmly walked to his place hitting slowly and steadily his triangle for directions. Of course, that moment of silence was then followed by a new general laugh.

'I think you hurt his feelings,' declared Putin with a spartan look, and another giggle.

'OK, that's enough, give me that shit!' It was Mattarella getting back to his hands the remote control of his negro. In a very diligently manner, he ordered ten Frangelico hazelnut liqueurs and a few plates with nibbles and informed his waiter that a child had accidentally picked up the communication device and had been playing with it. It wasn't an apology but something like that. The negro smiled and prepared the liqueurs. Nearly seven hours had passed since the Gs had started eating and drinking; by now they were fat enough to be sent to the slaughterhouse, oh pardon me; that's not what I meant. What I wanted to say was; seven hours had passed since those brilliant minds had met for the sake of mankind and what a wonderful job they were doing. They kept talking stupid rubbish that doesn't even deserve room in this book. I can only say that if I was to put Karl Pilkington in the same room with those 11, Karl would look like a philosopher. Sometimes I think what this world needs to be a better place is to clone Karl, or as he would say: - '…You know, the way that we have kids and stuff. It'd be good if what happened was, to control it, a man and a woman, right, they're born and that, they enjoy their life, they learn a lot. They live to be about seventy-eight by that point…You've done it all now. So I've had my innings, I live to be seventy-eight, but then, just as you die, you have a little baby inside you and, as you die, your life carries on'… Baby Pilkingtons, I dare say, may be the answer for salvation. Sometimes we overthink things too much, don't you agree? Evolution is so simple, beautiful, natural and hopeful, that is a fact; with us all being made out of the same matter and concept, how can we be so twisted and sad? Why do so few of us gain and lose reasoning to understand the meaning of life? How many times have you thought about what being alive really means? Do you understand what life is? Don't expect me to tell you just now. Maybe in another book I'll tell you what I think life is, but for now my best advice is: get out there and live it! You will never understand it if you don't experience it by yourself. There's nothing wrong in making mistakes; not learning from them is the acquiescence blunder.

'Very well, my cocksuckers, shall we do this shit?' Donald wanted attention…'Old MacDonald had a farm, you know the rest.'

Guterres intervened. He tried to get up. Forget about that, he sat again. His speech wasn't very clear by now. The THC had clouded his reasoning. All of them were just a little bit gloomy by now, let's be fair; they are special, but there's only so much drugs a human body can take until some senses start shutting down, but these were real people on a real mission, so they will not let us down. Guterres found his balance again by closing one of his eyes and a few of the others did the same; all good; time to carry on. 'My dear friends, I think, Ahaha, I feel it's time to, well, you know what I'm talking about, right?' Guterres said this pointing at the ceiling (pointing to the heavens above), trying to make some sense out of his words. He kept alternating one open eye with the other; it's actually a very good way to balance your body; close your right eye if your body starts falling to the left and the other way around works exactly the same way. 'Shall we start reading what we wrote earlier?' And all of them blindly grabbed their sheets from the table with a very drunk, stupid, happy smile on their faces. 'So, who wants to go first, no one, anyone?' By now, spotlight was like garlic for a vampire. 'Ahaha, we got shy all of a sudden?' No, mate, they are just too fucking pissed, I dare to say. 'All right, all right, so I'll go first and then maybe my old friend Juncker will go next?' Claude gave him a burped affirmative nod with the head. Guterres grabbed his sheet, closed one eye and opened the other and focused the best he could: 'Right; so; where was I again? Right; OK; so; I wrote down a few ideas but now that I look at this; huh; no, not this one; and this one? Oh no, no, ah yes, this is the one: right, my idea, and I have to say that I think it's amazing and it's very simple; the moon, right, has no gravity or atmosphere, right?'

'Well, yes, yes, you are right.' These were the general comments.

He carried on. 'OK; and space is infinite also, correct?'

'Yes, mate, it looks like that.'

'Right; and sheep, wool always grow back on sheep, right?' Everyone kept nodding affirmatively, but to be fair even I am starting to get lost in here.

'Just tell us what you have in mind, for fuck's sake!' Trump was getting impatient with this idea; maybe it is too complicated for him to think straight?

'OK OK OK; so: why don't we thread an infinite string and hook it to the moon? The way I see it, souls don't need oxygen to live, right? So why don't we just queue them up in space? They could easily be clipped to the string and just hang in there; we could then have our atmosphere back and think about the amazing view and quietude of space the souls would have; it's perfect, isn't it? But please, let's listen to your ideas.' There was a moment of silence. I think that Guterres really impressed the guys and let's be fair, what an imagination!

Trump raised his hand, he wanted to be next. Claude didn't mind and Donald carried on: 'Well, all right, well, your idea, my friend, I can only say that you put a lot of thought into that one. However, I have a much better one: my friends, bear in mind that Earth is like a casino; mankind is given numerous games they can choose from in order to achieve their dreams or the lack of them, what in a way suits our needs in perfection; since the loss of the slavery monopoly, you know how hard it has become to rule people; I know that I was elected by free man but the reality is that we can never trust what united people can decide next; too much freedom can be a pain. So, where was I again? Oh yes; gambling; casino games and people are much closely related also with the concept of justice, right?' At this point, everyone was getting a bit confused with this idea; that could be noticed looking at the frequency all of them closed and opened one eye trying to focus. Trump carried on in a very expressive way talking with his hands as if he was scaling concepts: 'So, on one hand we have justice and on the other hand we have gambling.' His hands levelled on an equal imaginary line. 'Right?' They all nodded with their heads up and down.

'So, if we put this in perspective, what is Heaven and what is Hell – a game of chance, right? Now, my dear friends, prepare yourselves for my idea,' He opened his arms and raised them up in the air creating a moment of suspense before declaring his idea: 'The Wheel of Destiny!' Silence. Everyone kept looking at him trying to focus on just one Trump instead of two and he went again like a priest shouting Alleluia inside a church: 'The Wheel of Destiny!' No reactions; again: 'The Wheel of Destiny! Oh, for fuck's sake, anyone getting my idea? All right, I'll explain it to you, you fucking drunken retards. OK; so; people live and then they die, right? After that they move on to the Limbo queuing up and in line waiting for a final judgment moment that will tell them which door to go knock on before you are given reincarnation or a duty in the skies above, or whatever, right? That takes time and having Jesus in Heaven may turn things kind of partial; all of us know how soft his heart is and how he preaches forgiveness and other crap; that is not fair, so,' and he shouts again: 'The Wheel of Destiny! People queue up, right? So, now imagine a triangle having at one angle Heaven, at the other Hell and finally at the last angle we place a Wheel of Destiny with cheeses alternating between Heaven, Hell and extermination; brilliant, right? Oh, and naturally we will not need to worry with the fate of our relatives and friends because like in any good old casino, not only the odds are on the house, but also the Wheel can be tempered by us for any urgent interest or friendly requests. What do you think? Amazing idea, is it not? I bet none of you cocksuckers will come up with one better than this.' Trump sat on the sofa confident with a clown smile on his face having all the other Gs staring at him the same way a donkey would look at a picture of a haystack printed on a wall and thinks: hum, what sort of witchcraft is this shit?

'Right; yes; that's a wonderful idea; yes; the electric eel and shit; so, who is next now; anyone; please?' Guterres was a bit confused by now. It had been a very exhausting day for all of them, but the crusaders would not give up, but to make this moment even more confusing the Samurai raised his hand; Shinzō will talk now:

'Thank you, my friends. Before I speak about my idea I would like to state that God is to blame for all this mess; your God and his selfishness; but that is your problem and the only reason I'm here is only for the sake of the financial stability of our markets.' Shinzō was sitting on the sofa in a very shaky straight yoga position, trying to look serious; he carried on confident: 'I have a very easy solution for your problem; as you know, my people doesn't have the same beliefs as yours,' yellow smile in his face, 'I would therefore say that small-minded God, small-minded people; ahaha!' Naturally, no one was able to make any judgments at this point. 'My friends, as you should know, the Japanese people believe in several different deities. We have a religion called Shinto, inspired in my name,' – I'm sure it was, for fuck's sake; drugs and alcohol – 'we are like the Christians, eternal. The twist, for the better in our faith is that we have several other worlds waiting for us on the other side once we abandon Earth. I can give you the example of Takamanohara, Yomi and Tokoyo, just to start with.'

'Pocoyo? Did you say Pocoyo? Isn't that a Spanish cartoon for children?' asked Guterres a bit confused.

'Most likely, yes; that or some other rubbish Japanese hentai production, ahaha...' mocked Trump with a big laugh.

Shinzô closed both eyes and then opened one, hoping to understand what they were both talking about. 'What? No, maybe, I don't know what you are talking about and it doesn't matter. Please allow me to explain my idea. I did not interrupt you guys when you spoke, did I?' They agreed and allowed the little Japanese fellow to carry on. 'Like I was saying, our future is not limited to one

Heaven and one Hell; plenty of room for every soul or spirit. So, now, stay with me: what I can do is contact my gods and ask them if it is all right to accommodate a percentage of your souls. I can assure you that they will say yes, with one very simple condition, of course.'

'Oh really, and what will that condition be, learn how to eat with chop sticks? Can someone pass me the metal triangle? I want to order some sushi; ahaha,' ridiculed Guterres; such a funny guy. 'Ahaha! Are you sure politics is your thing? Maybe you should join the circus!' An awkward moment of silence followed by a general laugh; friendship is a beautiful concept. 'Please carry on, my friend,' declared Guterres with a friendly smile balanced on his right eye.

'Thank you. Like I was saying; one simple condition: you Christians will have to accept our faith by denying and abjuring yours.' Silence.

'OK, fair enough; why not? I don't think God would be very pleased with your idea, but anyway, we still have a few more ideas to hear and from those we have to choose a couple...OK; what was I saying? What were you saying? Oh, fuck it! Give me triangle, please! Who is next, anyone?' Guterres ordered ten glasses of Port and another ten coffees. 'Come on, guys, it's getting late! Let's get this shit done so we can party after!'

Merkel raised her hand; uh, scary. 'I have an idea! I have an idea!' Whatever she had written on her sheet earlier made no sense anymore, I guess. 'All right; Ahaha! No, no, yes, yes, ahaha! One second; I can do it; ahaha!' Whatever she had to say, had no doubt caused a big impression on everyone; all of them were laughing with a stupid face. You know when you laugh at something, but you didn't get the reason why you are laughing? That's exactly what they were doing. For fuck's sake! Let's laugh along as well: Ahaha; ahaha! 'Wait, wait, oh my God, I'm going to pee myself; ahaha!'

'Come on, woman, just spit it out!'

'OK, listen…'

For fuck's sake, what the fuck will she say? Whatever she has in mind will have to wait for another chapter; now it's time to go back in time; Heaven, 1999.

CHAPTER 14

The tree of ignorance

'In the name of my husband, is that what I think it is? But how is possible? How in his name did you get your hands on this, and how does he not know about it?' Mary was naturally overwhelmed with that wonder, the Book of Destiny. Father Cruz was lost. He wanted to tell her the whole truth, but he knew that it was a secret he could not unveil.

'My dear lady, I beg of you not to ask me that question. I don't want to put you in the same place I was left a few years ago. In the name of your son, please never mention this to anyone because even his balance may be at risk.'

'For fuck's sake, Father, what have you done? I don't want to do this anymore! Take me out of here now!' Mary, like any mother, could bear the weight of the world on her back, but if her child is at risk, she will turn that world upside down or kick it away to protect him. 'This is wrong, Father. What if my husband is seeing us now?'

'No, my lady, he will not; everything is going to be fine. Please come over here, Mary,' and he opened the book at a specific page, 'please read it.'

Mary was confused. She wanted to leave that place but at the same time she was too curious. She went near the book and read the paragraph Cruz pointed to with his finger. She read slowly and carefully and then looked at the saint and said: 'In his name, what does this mean, Father? This can't be right. This is not possible. Father, who wrote this book, it was my husband, wasn't it?'

'I don't know, my sweetheart; I have been reading this book exhaustively for the last year and I still haven't found an answer for that question myself.'

'But how can this be, Father? How can we be here now if nothing really exists, Father? What does he mean with it?'

'I don't think that was what he meant, my lady,' and he read a short sentence from that paragraph: ' "…the day you see your God falling down on your feet you will understand how misled you were from the beginning and you will finally find your unity within multiplicity."' Well, let's be fair; this is a dodgy one; unity, within multiplicity; singularity, complexity, atoms, molecules…even I am getting troubled with this Book of Destiny; was it God who wrote it, or some primordial Einstein? Is that it then? Are we all just a talking feature of the universe? What are we in the end; stars with a different appearance and motion, what?

Father Cruz carried on his thoughts, streaming ideas from a place far away from his own understanding: 'Unfortunately, I can't ask your husband if he is the real author of this book, but I know from a reliable source that he had it with him until he got rid of it and destroyed it; at least, he thinks he did. In his name what I can say is that after reading it several times I have no doubts that he is part of it like we all are. What I can deduce from this book is that we are indeed part of something much more powerful than our religion. It seems, according to this book that neither faith nor the laws of the universe command our future, but I can't yet understand what rules us. It also mentions numerous events that have happened on Earth since the beginning of days…' Pardon, I need to interfere here before Mary will; does anyone understand what Cruz is saying?

Now I'll let Mary talk: 'For fuck's sake, Father Cruz, did you lose your mind? I can't understand what you are saying! Were you smoking marijuana with them at the party before you met with me? I'll tell you what, Father, I don't care anymore about who wrote that book or what that book says, it's just rubbish! I know who created the universe and mankind and whatever is written in there is just pure nonsense. You say that book mentions past events, don't you? Hello! Doesn't that ring you any bells? Maybe it's because it's not about prophecies, but a record of past events, and probably a bad one too. Who gave you that book, Father? I need to know! If you don't tell me who gave you this book, I will tell my husband you have it, fair enough?' Oops; Mary was suddenly very confident in her words. You know how addicted people react when they are told they are dependent on a certain substance? Exactly; everything is fine and I'm not dependent and I can quit any time I want and this and that. Father Cruz had no choice now; he would have to tell her who had given him that book. He resigned to Mary's powerful arguments: blackmail.

'It was a monkey.'

'Pardon? Say that again, a monkey? Oh, this story is getting better by the minute, a monkey, Father?'

'Yes. He found it buried in the jungle of Africa here in Heaven and brought it to me.'

Mary started laughing copiously. 'Really, and did he tell you also that it had been my husband writing it? You speak monkey language now, do you, Father? Ahaha! For fuck's sake, Cruz, anyone could have buried that book in there, even the Devil himself, for what I care. How many parties have we had together in Africa?'

'No, Mary, this book is different from another book I read before; this book has a reference to M. and A. and their birthdays and their Christian numbers, and...'

'And what, Cruz? I can't believe you!' Mary cut short his speech and carried on in a patronising way. 'So, a monkey found a book in the woods and gave it to you; you read it and thought it had been my husband writing it? But you actually are just making assumptions based on a few facts written in this book that coincide with our reality and based on that you decided to give a body to a legend spread here in Heaven about a mysterious Book of Destiny, was that it, Cruz? In the name of our love for Him, how could you be deceived so easily?'

'Well, not quite like that, because if you read this book, you will...'

'Stop, Cruz!' She shut him up again. 'I'll tell you what I think, Father: maybe it was another monkey that spread the legend. For fuck's sake, Cruz, this story is ridiculous. Do your magic tricks, and let me out of here, please.'

Cruz felt embarrassed and mumbled a few words that hid the book again and opened the secret door leading back to the saints' library. And as for me, I can only apologise, my dear readers, for the fact that you had to read around 500 words leading to another dead end in this story. The world is falling apart in the future and I wasted my time with a non-verified source. I promise I wasn't aware that Father Cruz had been given the Book of Destiny by a monkey; I'm not saying with that the Virgin Mary is totally right but, come on, maybe this Book of Destiny is nothing more than the Bible after all; legends created by monkeys. Father Cruz sat down with Mary in absolute silence. Mary had a triumphant smile on her face. Her husband was still the ultimate God. Her faith had been shaken temporarily probably because she was annoyed with what was going on in the savannah of Africa. I guess every woman feels the same when you see your love getting drunk and making a fool of himself, right? Mary broke the ice, again in a milder condescending speech.

'Look, Father, let's forget about this story; your secret is safe with me; I promise you. Why don't we go back to your dream and to the book of numbers? I'm sure we will find a way to sort out this mess. Let's be pragmatic and work with real facts.' and she summarised the truths briefly: 'No final judgment day; an empty Heaven; souls hanging lost in the Limbo; the Death Line; M.; A.; 5; 8; 13; and your dream; correct?'

'Yes, but the book says…'

'For fuck's sake, Father! Forget that fucking book!' Uh, you better forget about that book, Father; maybe you can introduce an idea without telling her about it, what do you think? I don't think Cruz can hear me, but I need to admit that I am curious about what was written in that book about M. and A. Oh, well, perhaps in another story. Mary had a machine gun look. Oh, she will definitely fire a good round over him if he doesn't shut up with that story. Cruz may look a bit naïve by now, but he is neither stupid nor inexperienced. He knew he had lost that battle but not the war and he even indulged her with some false honey.

'Fair enough, my lady, you are right, and I was wrong; you know how I love books and how I engage with words and ideas; I apologise. Let's forget that story and move on, as you said. Mankind needs our help. You are totally right; yes, I was wrong and I'm very sorry for that, Mary.' And there you go; magic; if half the men in this world could understand how saying sorry is important in a relationship, maybe, divorce rate, you will finally decrease. Pride should just be an annual show on the streets of

Brighton or a book by Jane Austen. Mary's pride had been soothed with Cruz's prejudice. She was feeling like the fucking queen of the universe; I guess she is.

The Virgin started talking very expressively with her hands reminding one of the Queen of England waving to her rustics. 'Never mind, my friend. Let's put that behind our backs. Tell me, Father, how will be able to bring people here to Heaven without a final judgment day? I mean, I want to help everyone, but how will we identify the black sheep in our flock without judging them? We can't just take their word as honest; who will judge them and how will we convince my husband doing that? Oh, Father, I'm so lost here. Tell more about your dream, please.'

Cruz focused his mind, checking inside his soul for all the details of his dream and: 'Like I told you under the Tree of Knowledge, my dream wasn't very clear, but allow me a few moments. Well, we were flying on a phoenix showing us the souls inside the Earth's atmosphere and I remember now that there were two distinct queues at the portal heading to the upper world...'

'That is most definitely the result of our priests' triage on Earth; that's why you saw two queues; one coming to Heaven and the other going to Hell; it makes sense, but it doesn't mean it's accurate. Please carry on,' said Mary.

'Yes, perhaps you are right. Like I was saying I saw the mist of souls and now I recall that there was one soul standing alone between the queues exactly at the beginning, creating a third queue; yes, I'm sure of that and maybe that soul was A. It makes sense now. It cannot be M. because we still don't have any records about his death.'

Mary intervened again. 'Very well, Father, that part of the third queue doesn't make sense, but it was just a dream, so, moving on, and you said you saw yourself dropping two different wooden objects down to Earth; probably you were sending them to M.'

'Yes, that's true too,' said Cruz showing the Virgin the wooden frame and the wooden slate he carried with him. Father Cruz wanted to tell Mary how the third queue made sense, but for that he would have to mention the Book of Destiny once more. There was, in fact, a third door leading to an unknown place at the upper level. Cruz focused his eyes on the Virgin but behind the scenes his soul was rushing an idea that would allow him to take Mary to the place mentioned in the book. After a few seconds, pretending he was thinking about what Mary had said he spoke with a very concerned and friendly tone of voice, 'I do apologise, My Lady, and I'm naturally worried about all this, but I can't stop thinking about the lunch in the savannahs of Africa; I'm not bothered with your husband, the saints, the fallen ones or even the animals because they can take care of themselves, but I do worry about your son; you know how bad he is with alcohol and drugs...maybe we could check on him and carry on talking on the way there?' Mary nodded yes with her head and just in case there was some sort of consciousness at the savannahs of Africa, they both put on their aluminium hats. Cruz led the way outside taking them to the portal between planes positioned at the centre of the bifurcation of the two paths: one leading to Heaven and the other turning left towards Hell. When they got there, Cruz deliberately dropped the key of his room on the floor covered with leaves from the trees paralleling the two paths. Luckily for him the key disappeared and just as he anticipated he had to remove a few layers of leaves to find it, and it was with great astonishment that Mary saw the same pattern of the other two paths unveiling underneath the leaves.

'Did you see that, Father?' Mary asked a bit confused.

'Did I see what, my lady?' Cruz was acting. He knew the path was there. The Book of Destiny mentioned it several times. Mary used her hands to reveal a typical Portuguese sidewalk made with small square polished rocks forming a strange lookalike patchwork. What looked like a mess of random white and black polished rocks was in fact binary code; I can't tell you what is written in there for now because the path is not cleared in its all extent.

'What's going on here, Father? What is this? Did you know anything about this? Does my husband know about this? Where is this leading to?

'No, Mary, I promised you I don't know anything about this.' Cruz was talking with his fingers crossed behind his back and it's a fact that he had heard of the existence of a third sidewalk but he never had the chance to investigate it; she was out of her mind.

'Give me that stick over there, Father, now! And help me with this, will you, for fuck's sake, Father!' Her heartbeat was out of control. She quickly cleared a straight line of leaves stopping at the base of an old large oak tree. If you imagine the outline of a V shape made by the other two paths leading to the other gates; inside the V form there was a shy garden without plants or grass covered with leaves and a single oak tree could be seen at its centre: the path was shorter than the other two and vanished at the base of the tree. 'How is it possible that no one has ever seen this, Father?'

'I don't know, Mary, and now that I think about it, I can't ever see anyone stepping on this ground; this piece of land between Heaven and Hell is known as neutral ground; it is said that any soul that steps on it will turn into nothing and why would saints and gods wish to be here in such a desolate little garden?'

'Oh really, and who told you that story, Father, another one of your monkey friends?'

'No, my lady, that's written in the book of laws regarding the use of the neutral land, at the exit of the portal coming from Earth. God and the Devil agreed on that around 2,000 years ago.'

'Oh, really? Fair enough. But does it mention anything about this path and why is this oak tree here?'

'No, there's no mention about this.'

Mary followed by inspecting the oak tree going around it: normal oak tree. The Virgin stretched her arm and gently touched the bark with her hand: 'Ah!' she screamed; at the same time all her body was electrocuted with a low voltage making her fall on the ground on top of a small object that clicked with her weight on it; it sounded like a personal mine click but she didn't blow up; instead the sound of metal cranks could now be heard working in an unidentified place. 'For fuck's sake, what the fuck is going on here? What is this, Father?'

'I don't know, my lady!' Cruz quickly helped her stand up and they both stepped back a few feet from the tree in fear, listening in disbelief to the clicks and creaks of cranks that sounded as coming from underneath them. Slowly magic or a greater design occurred in front of their eyes; the initial V shape outside earth's portal transformed into an E shape, leading now to a new destination; the leaves covering the central path to the oak tree were magically swiped aside, unveiling the full pattern of the sidewalk; a small yellow button could now be seen where Mary had tripped and finally the trunk of the tree opened like a door exposing inside a dark tunnel with a small light at its end. Mary and Cruz looked at each other terrified and in incredulity and in a motion that I can only show by giving you the image of Keanu Reeves dodging bullets during *The Matrix*; the same way both of them moved towards the yellow button; pressed it again and came back to the angle of the initial V-shaped path. They were both petrified in total silence staring at the oak tree.

'What the fuck just happened here, Father? And please don't tell me that this is mentioned in that Book of

Destiny...' Mary whispered, still in shock and unable to move a muscle.

Cruz didn't know what to say. This was, in fact, mentioned in the book found by the monkey, but he tried his luck anyway. 'I cannot tell you what you don't want to hear, My Lady.'

Mary swallowed dry pride and answered with a plain, hollow tone of voice, still entranced by the oak tree. 'Listen, Father, I don't know what to think anymore. I believe in my husband and whatever this means it will not shake my faith in him or in my son's religion, but we need to know what this means, Father; by whom and with what intent was this third path created? That worries me beyond my understanding; can this endanger the balance of our world? Where does that tunnel lead and why couldn't I touch it? You need to tell me what that damned book says about this shit, Cruz. Is this related with what will happen on Earth after my husband's and the Devil's crazy ideas? Is this connected with M. and A.? Is that why you saw three separate queues in your dream? Please, Father, you need to tell me everything you know about this third door.'

Father Cruz had to tell Mary what he knew, but how to explain to a child that it's time for him to stop playing his favourite game because it's time to study maths?

Cruz was as overwhelmed with what had just happened as Mary was; just because he had read about it in a book doesn't mean he could more sense out of it then her. He started digging inside his soul something to say that would make some sense for both of them and then in a lost speech he started: 'Just for the sake of theorising about what just happened here, now and about the things I read in the Book of Destiny, do you remember, Mary, when you had to tell Joseph that you were pregnant? Can you imagine what his first reaction must have been?'

Jesus's conception and birth was always one of those subjects that irritated the Virgin, but I guess, in front of the events that had occurred recently, she could only answer what she did: 'Yes, Father. I can imagine he must have had many doubts and must have felt a bit disappointed at me and at the world, but I cleared that with him and everyone knows that I had nothing to do with it. I just happen to be the chosen one by God as the vehicle of hope…'

'Yes, everybody knows that, my lady; thank you for indulging me with your words of understanding. That was exactly what I was expecting from you in a troubled and grey moment like the one we are in now.' He paused for a few seconds and then carried on talking, tilting his head up and fixing his eyes on the blue sky above. 'Naturally,

Mary, I'm not saying that the things written in the Book of Destiny will have the same fate as yours or your son's religion had after that initial blurry start. The things written in that book were not prophecies or Bibles about religion, but the reality was that, more and more, the sentences handwritten inside were becoming true.' Cruz carried on with a very focused and slow speech: 'This door is mentioned in that book, Mary, the same way, God, you and your son are.'

Mary was listening to Cruz in disbelief and a watery brightness woke up in her eyes. She had to interject: 'Does the book mention the end of Christianity, Father?'

'No, Mary. It doesn't talk about the end of Christianity or any other religion, but it does say that the third door will lead us to a new way of thinking. Very well, my lady, if you are really and truly interested in knowing what the book says, I can try to summarise it briefly; I'm assuming we have plenty of time to talk about it because the book also talks about something like this, that a party in Heaven will end with the intrusion of a saint and a Virgin – I'm guessing those are us – and we are still here, so, we should be fine.'

Mary swelled dry again and whispered in a very resigned, fainted way, 'For fuck's sake, Father, just tell me what that dammed book says about all of this. I can't take it anymore.'

Father Cruz looked at her and felt she needed a hug just as every woman in this twisted world needs. She needed reassurance that she was still there in that moment; that she wasn't just a vain projection of a being. The worst thing a man can do is seeing a woman suffering in despair and not doing something about it and just pretend she is invisible or that whatever she has will disappear same way it appeared, because it will not; whenever we do that, that's exactly what they will turn into; invisibility. How can we long for love and attention when we treat women like objects abandoned still on a shelf building dust inside their souls? Why do we only show courtesy and caring when they lie down on a bed with us? Why do we treat women as things that we use and dispose of depending on our needs? Father Cruz opened his arms wide open and offered her a hug before he started talking again. Mary welcomed that attitude as a glass of water given to a European lost in the Saharan desert. She remained in his breathing profoundly until she felt the fear of ignorance disappear.

She then released Cruz's body and stepping back at arm's length, she held his hands and looking him straight in the eyes said: 'Give it to me, Father.'

Being a saint but also a man, Cruz changed colour and felt a bit embarrassed; who wouldn't, but his experience told him that Mary was just troubled and what she really wanted to say was something like, 'Tell me, Father' and so he did: 'Mary, my lady, this book talks about the past, the present and the future. It talks also about change, love and freedom.' Cruz was talking in very confident manner, like a priest lecturing his flock with a paused and calm tone of a messiah. He proceeded: 'Throughout history, many civilisations have claimed their own gods with their own religions; our God. In all his omnipotence he allowed that to happen because he gave us all free will and no matter what our individual choices are, he would judge us together during the final judgment day; then, our Lord, the creator of all things would separate the black sheep from the true believers and send them to Hell…'

'Yes, Father, I know that. Every fucking Christian knows that. Can you tell me something I don't know, for fuck's sake!' Mary was acting as a bipolar; her mood was going up and down like a roller-coaster. For fuck's sake, even I am starting to get annoyed with Father Cruz, are you not? Just let us know what the fuck is in that book that matters so much! What's going on at the savannahs of Africa? What are the G10 doing in this exact moment? Where is

António? What happened to M. at the Royal Pavilion Gardens in Brighton? Why the door? What will happen? So many questions, isn't this frustrating? Are you not irritated with all this, just like me and Mary? Are you? Good. I'm happy if you are, because it means that I've accomplished what the true use of any art should be: provoking emotions. Let me assure you that if you are still reading this book, this story will not let you down and will, as I hope, fill your soul with something different and new, for there's no one in the universe like me. What that new knowledge will be, maybe I mentioned it already, and perhaps I haven't. It can be that everything will make more sense in the end and perhaps it won't. My job is not to serve you the facts on a plate as an easy meal. My role is to give you the ingredients and let you cook them as you wish. For now, let's go back to the three gates in the upper world and listen to what Father Cruz has to say about this Book of Destiny and how they will put together the pieces of this crazy puzzle, and do not worry if I don't mention it in this chapter, maybe, perhaps it's just because I want your blood to start boiling inside your cold hearts.

Cruz started talking in a patronising way to a Mary with the expression of a spoiled child. 'Mary, you know me well. You know that if I'm talking about these matters, it's because I need to create a frame for the abstract concepts I'm about to tell you' – introspective pause – 'as I was saying, final judgment day; we know now that there will not exist such a day, unless your husband changes his mind and we both know how small the probability is of that happening. The book talks about this as well. It says also that the third door was created before both your husband and the Devil made that decision; it says the third door was created by one singularity of will – and I don't understand what that means. It does not say where it leads or who will cross it first or last, but I believe now that M. and A. are part of it, but I don't know how. In the book it is mentioned that from the earth a hollow solution for the souls hanging in the Limbo will arrive; something about ten individuals gathering together and delivering a message to your husband, but it does not say what that key is. It talks about saints creating demons and demons creating saints and doors that will close and doors that will never close again…'

'For fuck's sake, Cruz! What the fuck are you talking about, saints, demons, doors? Can you stop with these fucking riddles!'

'No, Mary, it's not me, this is exactly how the books puts it.' Mary was possessed with ignorance again and Father Cruz tried to make some sense out of what he was saying: 'If you think about it, Mary...'

'Think about what, Father, saints and demons working together, for what?' She was blinded by fury.

Cruz pushed harder: 'Well, my lady, what is happening right now at the savannahs of Africa, don't we have saints and demons working together in hopes of reaching a common goal?' They both went silent for a while and then Mary said in a less angry manner: 'Well, in a way you are right, but in my husband's name I don't understand anything anymore. Who creates saints and demons, is that not a human design?' Another moment of silence. 'My husband needs to know about this, Father! We need to know if he is responsible for that book. Nothing makes more sense any longer and all this is scaring me, Father. I fear we will not be able to sort out any of this shit. We need to tell him.'

Surprisingly, or maybe because his faith had been shaken, he answered, 'Yes, you are right, my lady.'

Exactly at this moment they heard a voice inside their heads: 'What the fuck have you been talking about?' It was God.

'Yep; that crazy story of you two got me interested as well,' said the Devil with a laugh.

Mary and Cruz never noticed it, but she had lost her hat when she was electrocuted by the old oak tree and Cruz's had fallen when he helped her recuperating from it. God damn it! I guess that Cruz's earlier assumption that God was too drunk and high to listen to everyone's thoughts was wrong. He forgot in his guess that God had been sharing milk with the Devil for the last couple of hours. Oh well, there's no way of running out of it now.

A strident voice trembled inside their souls: 'Both of you stay exactly where you are! I and my mate will be with you very shortly.' After this the same voice echoed everywhere in Africa: 'This shit is over! Everyone cleaning after themselves, you fucking monkeys!' No doubt the milk had cleaned his blood and his mind. God and the Devil went to the portal and crossed it still wearing their expensive fancy suits. Mary and Cruz felt like digging a hole in the ground and sticking their heads in it very deep. They both arrived with a freezing look, staring at the other two without saying anything and after they moved their attention towards the old oak tree.

'What do you think?' asked the Devil.

'I don't know,' answered God. A graveyard silence conquered the atmosphere and even the blue skies above acquired greyish tones. Without moving his attention from the oak tree, God ordered Cruz to go fetch the book the monkey had given to him, told Mary to stay where she was and demanded Jesus's presence in there as well. Jesus was helping the monkeys tidying up the mess left in Africa. He showed up at the same time Cruz came with the Book of Destiny. Jesus went to stay with his mother who looked as helpless as a wet cat.

CHAPTER 15

The raise up day

Merkel couldn't stop laughing. The negro showed up again with ten glasses of Port leaving the tray on the table with an impressive accuracy. The laughing stopped temporarily whilst they watched him doing it and going back to the bar by hitting the metal adaptor for directions. Once more they cheered up for some non-audible cause. Merkel was sitting between Trump and Putin keeping her balance by hanging on to their cocks – over the jeans, naturally. I think that both of them were getting a bit excited because Putin said: 'Please carry on' – and Trump added: 'Yes, please, let us know how you want it; I mean, tell us your idea, please.'

Merkel giggled and moaned a little bit at the same time as she gave a harder squeeze on both of them; she then calmed down and started talking: 'Very well, cocksuckers, I will talk now. Firstly, I would like to congratulate you guhys for your amazing ideas, but I have most definitely a much better one.' Even in her disgraceful condition she acquired a sudden imperial appearance, I wonder why? 'My dear friends, let's be pragmatic about this subject; apart from our relatives that have died, what do we know about the rest of the souls; who are they for us all and what good can they bring us? Is it really our job worrying about that? Is that not the job of priests, here on Earth and the job of God and the Devil in the other world? Is it not our role the balance of economies and their respective productivity? Is that not what really matters in society?' Merkel grabbed the attention of everyone with their questions; she carried on: 'Has God ever helped us here on Earth? Did he ever sit down at a table with us and explain to us simple things, like terrorism and war being ultimately fundamental for the fluctuations of markets and for our business?'

'Well, he was never opposed to a good war,' said Trump being interrupted straight away by Merkel:

'Fuck off, Trump! He never opposed anything good or bad, and you know well that it had to be us figuring out that bad things are the real engine of our society! Do you want to know what I think? I think that the truth is that he doesn't bother, he never cared about us; and if he doesn't give a shit, why should we help him with his fucking problem?' she said with a plain evilest hollow tone and made a pause for a few seconds, allowing everyone a moment of reflexion. 'And do you know why he doesn't care? Because he is a selfish bastard just like everyone inside this room. This crazy story about what he did with the Devil just shows that; none of them fucking care about us! And then he turns down on us asking for help? This is fucking ridiculous!'

Guterres decided to intervene in a very false diplomatic way, balancing himself on the sofa by opening and closing one eye at the time (maybe he wasn't very happy with the terms of the Dutch bank regarding the external Portuguese debt): 'Very well, Merkel. I think we all understood your points and we all naturally respect them, but we were asked by Him to deliver a solution for all this mess and in His name, that's what we will do so, please, can you stop with this bullshit and just let us know what your idea is? And if you don't want to do it, it's fine, I don't think anyone in this room will take you wrong for that.'

Merkel renewed her confidence with Guterres's words. 'Fair enough, you prick. My friends, we all know this world has its days counted. I'm not even going to bother talking about climate changes, wars, diseases, natural resources and shit like that; I'm talking about the inevitable extinctions of stars and planets and I'm sure you very well know what I'm talking about. How many billions have we swiped out from the general population with our taxes so we could fund our space investigation, and what does God do about that?' Another moment of silence. 'Nothing! Fucking nothing! Why doesn't he just hand us another planet like this one? I'm sure he has plenty of planets similar to Earth in this immense universe and even if he doesn't, why not create one? How many days did it take him to create the fucking cosmos?'

Trump and Guterres raised their hands as if they were at elementary school. Before Guterres had time to show off a bit, the true showman shouted: '144 hours!'

And before Merkel had the chance to say 'Yes you are right', Guterres said: 'Nope! It was not! God created the universe in 184 hours; ahaha!'

'Pardon me, my friend António; I'm not Christian but I know the story told in the Bible and according to it, everything was, in fact, created in six days; 24 hours per day times six; you just need to do the maths,' declared Shinzô.

Guterres laughed even more and then he added: 'Ahaha! God worked overnight too! Ahaha!'

Everyone tried to make some sense out of what he had just said, but only Merkel answered: 'Ahaha, very funny, Guterres. That's a story about Hitler, is it not?' It was indeed. It's said that Hitler ordered his troops to pursue Jews 36 hours per day because there were too many of them. Anyway, when their captains confronted him with the fact that one day has only 24 hours, he answered them that in that case they should pursue them overnight too. What a lovely story about Jews, Mr Guterres; but it doesn't surprise me because not only the Germans longed for an empire and were responsible for genocides. What have the Turks, the Chinese, the Italians, the Spanish, Portuguese, French, English, Russians, Americans and so on, what have they done? How different is a Christian from any other religion or a negro from a white, a yellow or a redskin? It's so fucking easy to point fingers at other nations, is it not? Maybe we should start looking at our bellies and our history first, before we start throwing rocks on others' sins, but that is a matter, I mean, shit for another fiction; and I will write it about some day; a lot of people out there are needing some enlightenment regarding moral values and hypocrisy. I guess, sometimes, I feel that it is still possible to change the world; what do you think? Do you think that we can change the world together, or are you just another number in a book believing that fighting is pointless and our fate is some sort of a great design from which we cannot run away?

Merkel initiated her monologue again: 'Fuck off, OK, Guterres; you and your stupid imperial jokes! Hitler had his reasons to put his troops working during the night; ahaha! Well, can I finish my line of thought before I finally introduce you to my idea?'

'By all means, my dear; I would just like to order another drink if you don't mind,' said Shinzō reaching for the metal triangle.

Merkel had a sudden rage attack, grabbed the metal triangle and hit it indiscriminately, repeatedly as she shouted at him and everyone in a very angry manner: 'No, you can't! No one is fucking asking for any more drinks until I finish my fucking thought!' She continually repeated the same sentence whilst hitting the triangle. Everyone had a stupid smile on their faces and decided to go quietly along with Merkel's sudden depression attack provoked by too many drinks and drugs. They all waited in silence until she came back to Earth and was ready to spit out her idea. At this point no one noticed it, but the negro abandoned his post and went to the bar. He then took a couple of things from one of his pockets and started preparing drinks for all of them. Poor man, he had been misled again. 'Very well; now that I made myself clear, may I carry on? I thought so; good. OK. Now I'm going to ask you; to whom do the souls belong? Huh? Have you thought about that? And if you are thinking that they belong to God or to the Devil, you are mistaken, and this is where my idea fits in. Stay with me; was the Earth not given to humans and other species and wasn't instinct and rationalism allied with the survival of the fit and free will also given   to us?'

' "The origin of Species by Means of Natural Selection or the Preservation of Favoured Races in the Struggle for life", is that what you mean?' asked May, reminding everyone of the role of the British in society.

'Yes, whatever, answered Merkel devaluing Darwin's work. 'Like I was saying: doesn't this mean that God gave us the planet to use it as we please and fuck it in the end?' The rest of the crowd wasn't yet quite sure where Merkel was heading with this speech, but a sense of sympathy could be seen on their expressions. Maybe she is right, they were thinking. 'Now I ask you again; and I'm not even talking of the souls already waiting in the Limbo, but to whom do you think that the ones hanging on the atmosphere belong?' (Silence) 'Don't you know? Well, let me tell you then: everything inside this planet and even out there in space belongs to us, my friends, so, if everything is ours, why should we help God? Why don't we just keep the souls and use them as exchange currency between Earth and the upper world? Another minute of silence only disrespected by the sound of the negro preparing what seemed to be ten cocktail drinks. 'Do you understand what I'm telling you? Interests and profit, my friend; that's what I'm talking about!' Merkel was finally ready to show her game: 'What I propose is to vacuum the souls back to Earth. There's plenty of room to keep them inside our Earth; there's plenty of room to keep them all here and use them in our favour; I say: let's demand from God a new planet. We can even allow him to choose its name, but for once in the history of mankind, let Him be the bitch!'

No one was quite sure what to say at this point, until Trump said: 'My dear, what you propose is no doubt an extraordinary idea, but how will we collect the souls from the atmosphere and how will we hide them from God?'

Before she had the chance of answering Putin raised his hand in a wobbly manner: 'Well, to be fair, there's a way of penetrating the atmosphere and the Death Line; one of my scientists made an amazing breakthrough...'

Trump changed, apparently, from completely drunk to completely sober: 'What the fuck are you saying? Did anyone else know about this shit?'

Putin gave him a clue when he fixed his open eye on Merkel's hand. 'What? You knew about this shit? You fake bitch!' yelled May at Merkel.

'What? Chill, you cocksucker. Did you not sell the Polish to us and to the Russians to put an end to the Second World War, huh? Chill out; moreover you wouldn't tell us anything either and it's not like we have a way of ending the Death Line; we can only cross a diameter the size of a fat cock; the size you would need to calm down.'

'Ahaha; fuck off, you Nazi!' answered May.

'The size of a fat cock, what do you mean?' asked Shinzō, probably worried with his own diameter.

'Yes, more or less the size of woman's wrist.'

'Keep dreaming; ahaha!' declared Mattarella.

'What? What do you mean?' replied Shinzō kind of upset.

'Hey; calm down, boys. Let's focus on the hole and not on the cock; can one of you explain to us what you are talking about, please?' said the diplomat. It was Putin's time to talk: 'I don't know what you guys have been doing since the Death Line showed up in our sky, but us Russians have been throwing all sorts of things at it ever since. The Germans have been helping us with their Zeppelins; floating at a very close and safe distance, we have tested all the objects and animals you can imagine, including humans. Everything vaporised, until one of my scientists came up with one theory that, maybe, if the Death Line had been created by the upper world, maybe holy items would be immune to it; after trying a few things we have in our possession something finally worked, and let me tell you in advance that it is pointless for any of you asking me how we have it because I will not tell...'

Trump was about to explode. The cold war games were back on, and it looked as if the Americans were losing it again. Trump's reddish and drunk look was plotting a way of robbing the Russians' plans again, just like in the good all days. He had to say something. 'You cocksucker and you, you bitch, how long were you keeping hiding this shit from us?! What's the fucking point of the G10?!' I think that Trump didn't cry when he shouted this because he felt embarrassed. The rest of the G10 members also gave one eye of disapproval, both to Putin and Merkel and wonkily waited for an explanation from them. The explanation came from Putin. Long nights of vodka gave him an edge of sobriety in that moment.

'Come on, guys, don't tell us all of you don't have your own side projects going on? I'm sure you do, and please rest assured that we were going to tell you all about it as soon as we had something more solid…'

'Yeah, sure, no doubts about that; well, I guess the right moment has arrived, so what are you waiting for?' Trump was possessed with envy. He frowned and stuck up his lips out in a very pouty expression. Again, the land of Superman and so many other heroes wasn't able to shine as it always should.

Merkel felt sympathetic and petted his jeans a few times before she started talking: 'Calm down. Very well, I'll explain everything. Like my friend Putin said, I hope you understand that it was not our intention hiding this from any of you; we were just waiting until we were sure what would actually work and that, my friends, is: the Holy Grail and the Spear of Longinus; I'll explain everything, OK? So, what was I saying? Ahaha; the cup and the stick, (hiccups) yes; so, like I was saying and you can correct me if I'm wrong' – another squeeze on Putin's pad – 'this scientist fused the tip of Longinus's knife, (hiccups) sword, oh fuck, whatever; he fused both things and then we glided one of our beautiful Zeppelins up to two feet of the Death Line; maybe less; and surprisingly when he pushed it up it did not vaporise. He went up and down, up and down; ahaha; and it worked. After this we tried to attach numerous materials including animals thinking that whatever was in contact with it would not vanish; unfortunately, that didn't work. Luckily for all of us, another of our scientists came up with the idea of drilling the inside of both objects and infiltrating a probe camera in it and *voilà*! It worked. My friends, for the first time in many days we managed to cross the Death Line and saw what is going on above. We finally took a glimpse into the afterlife and let me tell you something, it doesn't look much different from the Lord's death camps. No doubt God doesn't care much about his flock; everyone is pale and greyish over there, my friends.' Merkel's speech acquired a stupid spooky tone: 'Let me ask you something; when you think about a soul, how do you envision it?' The question was direct to Trump. He was caught by surprise. Two hard questions: thinking and soul.

He took a few moments before answering. 'Oh, for fuck's sake, really? I think of, I mean, oh fuck, I don't know.'

'Exactly, my friend,' declared Merkel and she carried on: 'Now I know how a soul looks like and I'm going to share it with you all; I was even lucky enough to see my grandfather between the other souls. Oh, my God, I'm so happy; he was there queuing with the rest, but he never saw me. None of them saw. It was an awful sight, to be fair. He looked exactly the same way the day he died, and he was wearing exactly the same clothes we dressed him in, bless him. His shape was also out of focus and his body had turned into a diffuse mist of shades of grey. All the other souls looked the same, like grey wheat waving in the fields. Do you know what that means?' More silence. The negro was preparing the seventh cocktail. 'No one, anyone? Fair enough, I understand that all of you must be very over-whelmed with what I just told you; I know. I will now go back to my idea; I don't want to confuse your little brains anymore, ahaha! From what we were allowed to see their bodies have shape, look the same but have no density, they are like smoke and this, my friends, means they can all be vacuumed by a very thin hose that we can fit inside Long-inus's lance. Because of that we can easily condense mil-lions of them using the same simple process of making cup-a-soups; stay with me, it's very simple, it's like turning milk into dried milk; gallons and gallons of souls dried and condensed into small aluminium sachets. And do not worry; our scientists assured us that the process is revers-ible. Moreover, everyone knows how aluminium foil works for God like kryptonite works for Superman. Why do you think we covered this room with aluminium; right?'

'Oh fuck, and the windows?' asked Macron in despair.

Shinzō got up very slowly trying to keep his balance and walked towards the windows in silence whilst everyone was still digesting what Merkel had said. Once he got there with a big smile on his face he touched what seemed to be the window, but it was not: 'Not only your God is capable of amazing things; REGZA GL1; the first 3D television without the need of wearing special glasses; with the best regards from my friends from Toshiba! What you have been seeing in here, my friends, is a live broadcasting of the outside; ahaha! Oh, for fuck's sake, anyone else in here has any more secrets to reveal? You knew about this shit, Guterres? Of course, you knew, you fucking asshole!'

'Can someone please give this man a pacifier?' said Guterres with a smile on his face. The negro was preparing the last cocktail.

Shinzō tumbled back to the sofa and Merkel took this chance to carry on. 'Like I was saying, God will never know what was said inside this room, so why don't we send him an email letting him know of our good intentions of keeping the souls here on Earth; without mentioning our real plan? Naturally, all the research we did was well disguised by aluminium, just in case he wasn't too busy playing his stupid games.' The atmosphere inside that room got heavy with a deadly silence; only the sound of stirring cocktails could be heard again.

'And I'm sure Jesus will soften his heart. Do you think that Jesus will not finally stand up for something after 2,000 years of promises? Come on, good people, what do you say? I'm sure that we still have a few more ideas under the hat, but I know that this is the jackpot! Why don't we just send this proposal and if he doesn't accept it, then we can think about something else tomorrow? I'm fucked for today, I think, ahaha.'

All of them were suddenly optimistic, so confident that the rest of the members of the G10 decided to go with it and fold their game and go with that plan. Everybody was actually getting very excited with this idea. Guterres looked at them and after having a silent approval he went to the computer on the desk placed against a nearby wall and quickly drafted an email explaining to God about their plan of vacuuming the souls from the atmosphere back to Earth and keeping them in a safe place until God sorts out the issue created by the non-existing final judgment. He even added that they could vacuum a few more million directly from the Limbo so God could have more time to think about it, giving him with that a bigger buffer. As a personal favour, the members of the G10 would like him to consider the creation of another planet similar to Earth for their descendants and also their beatification and a free pass to Heaven, avoiding like this hassle of Limbo and as a reward for their great job on Earth. Guterres followed by reading the email out loud for the rest of the crowd, who gave him thumbs up. Perfect. 'Kind regards from the G10' and pressed enter; in less than a second God had the email in his inbox. The subject was white smoke. God was busy playing call of duty. He mentally split his screen in two and accessed his mailbox with a laugh on his face. He didn't have to read because he knew what was coming. It turns out that the G10 forget to cover all the room in aluminium. The plug where the computer was connected had not been covered; silly mistake. What a bunch of drunken losers, ahaha! God quickly typed in the following message: 'My dear friends. It's with great excitement that I'm hearing news from you all. I can only say that I'm amazed with your good work and your abilities. I knew I made the right choice when I decided to put you in charge of Earth and the earthlings. I'm so proud of you all. Well done. I love your idea. I think it's time for you all to celebrate. I'll get back to you very soon so we can arrange the final details about how to extract the souls from the Limbo area as well. Once again, thank you very much, my dear friends.' He attaches an audio file; sends the email and carries playing his new game with a big smile on his face.

On Earth, Guterres was still balancing his body trying to find his way back to the sofa when an alert sound came from the computer. Again, he balanced himself back to the desk and read the mail in silence for a few seconds before announcing in a very enthusiastic manner: 'Game on, guys! He took the bait; ahaha.'

'What did I tell you, cocksuckers? We are perfectly isolated with this aluminium,' declared Merkel in triumph.

Euphoria took over the room in such a way that when Guterres mumbled, 'Oh, there's an attachment in his email; it's an audio file with the title "have a drink on me",' what the rest of the G10 heard was: 'bla, bla, bla, bla...' Guterres played the audio file but the chattering around silenced it and Guterres thought that maybe the file was corrupt. He went back to his seat and joined the celebration leaving the file on play. A lax atmosphere took over the place. The males started seeing the females as desirable steaks. An orgy was about to take place. Guterres spoke: 'I know what we need.' He opened the box and spilled coke all over the table and then grabbed the metallic triangle. Everything got suddenly blurry. Before Guterres played the triangle, the negro arrived with ten cocktails. Guterres had another sniff of coke and looked at the negro with a smile still holding the triangle: 'Fuck, this shit is good and efficient; this is amazing; you are all amazing,' he said, completely fucked. The waiter placed the tray with the drinks on the table and walked back to the bar where he started preparing one other drink. 'Come on, guys, let's celebrate! We fucking did it!'

Everyone was Goddamn Zen; the effect of the alcohol and the drugs had finally taken over their bodies and their souls; another drink was just what they needed; they all rose up the right arm with their cocktails and cheered up out loud: 'Spring Break!' They drunk everything in one go.

'This shit is good. What is this shit?'

'Yes, what is this? I never had anything like this.'

'Mine actually tastes bitter...' General comments. All of them got instantly dizzy and their breathing got heavy and hard.

'What is this cocksucker?' asked Trump for last.

'How am I supposed to know; wasn't it one of you who ordered this?'declared Guterres coughing.

'What the fuck do you mean? So, who was it?' tried to scream Merkel.

Guterres gave it a quick thought and ended up saying: 'Well, maybe it was God. I read you the email, didn't I? He left a PS telling us to have a drink on him and there was also an audio file with an imperceptible metallic cling... I told you about it, didn't I? If you were not listening, that's not my fucking problem, is it?'

'What the fuck are you saying?' An acute pain showed up inside their stomachs. 'You fucking asshole, can't you see what you have done?' Their pain increased severely; Merkel wanted to jump over the table and kill Guterres; she was the only one that understood what had just happened. Everyone knows when we do something wrong it stays with us forever like a shadow following our consciousness. We can try to forget about it, but it will always haunt us. With great difficulty she managed to say: 'He knows! Why would he offer us a drink and how could he know that drink had to be served by a blind man that answers to metallic clings, you fucking asshole?' She couldn't talk anymore, none of them could. For the next five minutes the most poisoning death played with their bodies; their vision started blurring; disorientation and excessive tearing came along with more excruciating pain until the moment they shifted to Limbo and faced their own wait. Once you get there, then you are completely lost because he doesn't care about you; he is busy playing other games. Fucking asshole was their last thoughts. Ten more alphas have failed, and soon better ones would take their place, for with changing comes big hope. God was in their souls all along because he was their light and they failed to imagine that he would be able to see through electricity; the energy that kept them connected to God even though he is playing stupid games all the time. See you later, sucker.

CHAPTER 16

Fusion

In Brighton, M. is found dead at the Royal Pavilion Gardens sitting down straight; with his back against an old tree with a fork deep in his heart. He was dead. Had his wallet still in the same place; he died holding it with left hand. What is the meaning of this shit? People live and people die and that's it; God doesn't care about it? Excuse me? What are you saying? Fuck, fuck, where the fuck am I? Huh shit, fucking headache. M. was feeling an overwhelming energy around him; it was like when you lose a leg or an arm, and your brain still plays the same record? Well, M. had no body now. Limbo is the medieval grounds; it's the place where only a few will go, the streamline of life. M. carried on: 'What the fuck, why can I feel this and not be dead, I must be dreaming? Yeah yeah, that's it. Of course! And maybe I'm dreaming and imagine if I was in coma on a bed? See, that gives you another option, this doesn't make any sense and dreaming, coma, just, no fuck, no fucking way.'

M. was inside the atmosphere with the idea of having a body that he couldn't feel and a mermaid male echoed throughout the atmosphere saying: 'Please keep turning around in slow motion. The extra use of more than your designated perimeter will put you back to the start of the line. Please squeeze where you can so you access the tunnel the Two Gates for the two doors for level 2. God loves you and the Devil hates you. Welcome to   Stage Two.'

'Ahaha this is nice. Like this dream. Fuck if someone wakes me from this dream, I will scream like a child the whole fucking day and I won't, and I won't take my pills; ahaha; carry on, M., nice dream.'

The voice echoed again between the very slow twisting shapes of belief, 'Your number is imprinted in your memory; please access your number for lottery day for our annual free pass for fusion moment. Fusion moment will decide your fate: door one, door two or particular and unicellular probability.'

'Oh, my God, this is the most amazing dream I ever had; please read your number now,' said M. feeling a smile. M. looked at his number and eight 76 13 17 and he smiled again; he remembered his father's date of death and when he added 7 plus 6 of his year of birth he said 13. 'I'm sure you are well, Father, and I promised I would see you again, so don't lose your faith until we meet again.' M.'s shape started increasing speed of rotation and M. having the most amazing dream in his life. Somewhere else in the atmosphere A., father of M., was twisting and thinking: tonight, what I want for dinner is steak; you know a rib or something like that. Number, what number? Wrist, what wrist? He heard the mermelodie, looked at his wrist and saw eight five 50 17 13 and said, 'I know this number: I miss you as well, my son. I know you are fine.' A. went back to the moment he had died and heard M. talking from somewhere. It's nice when you love someone, that no matter what, we always feel safe and happy when we are around them, is it not so? A. went back in time to a sunny rear patio in Portugal somewhere near the Atlantic Ocean where he was rebuilding a collapsed tunnel with his little boy many years ago. His shape started twisting faster too between the seamless lines of souls leading to the portal.

CHAPTER 17

Illusion

Everyone was gathered by the three gates. 'Very well, you and you fuck off near the entrance of that door on the tree,' said God to the demon, the saint and a few monkeys leading them the way with his arm; after he turned to Jesus, Cruz and his wife facing them from the front having the Devil on his right hand side. He looked at them for a few minutes reading them and then started patronising them with a slow melodic speech: 'Well. Needless to say that none of you three stooges know something about this, but someone did something wrong and we need to find out who it was and I can assure that I will show my mercy on you like I always have, but someone better step forward or today, my friend, here is reading you his Bible for a few years.' They were so scared. They were looking at God the same way a human would look up to a Titanosaurus, reduced to tiny little things like ants. They kept in silence facing the floor. 'Very well. Let's look at what we have here; a book that a monkey gave you; a book found in the savannahs; a tree that I have never seen in my eternity; a tree that can't be touched by me and has a door; a button that creates a new path and a new door...' God paused and looked at the Devil waiting for an answer; the Devil shrunk and gave no answer.

'And no final judgment day,' said the Virgin Mary shyly from her smallness.

'Yes, and no final judgment day,' repeated God. He followed with the line, 'Where exactly did the monkey find this book?'

'In the jungle past the savannah in the same area here, you my Lord, through your meetings and your parties,' answered Cruz.

God gave it a little bit more thought. 'There's only one way of sorting out this shit; we need to create the conditions for the prophecy in that book to be fulfilled. Only by bringing M. and A. to this place will we know what this means.'

'I was thinking about the same but I was thinking also about what we might create here, my friend; once they fuse and become only one, who will that new one be and what will happen to everything?' said the Devil with some concern.

'I know what you mean, but you and I should be able to take care of whatever comes; throw your demon, the saint and the monkeys through the door and let's hope for the best.'

The Devil met with the lab rats and told the demon to go first; he was confident he would go through and come back. That didn't happen. One after the other were electrocuted and left unconscious sleeping on the floor. Calmly, the Devil came back near frowning his eyebrow. God had watched what happened, but he didn't seem surprised about it. The Devil came out with a theory whilst God kept silent with the others. 'You know, I've been thinking about this book. You have accessed the same information as me, so what I'm going to tell you crossed your mind already.'

'Most definitely, but please indulge me because, to be fair, I'm not quite sure how we will fix this.'

'Thank you, my friend. I have been thinking about our parties in Africa.'

'What about it?' queried God.

'Well, how do you actually create the scenery? Is it all fake, or do you actually transport us there?'

'Oh, I see. Well, I guess that it really doesn't matter now; actually, the portal takes us there; I just hide us from the human eye and hide their presence the same way; why do ask?' questioned God.

'I'm just thinking; and in what time does that happen; you know what I mean; past, present or future?'

'To be fair, I'm not quite sure, but I guess it's in the present.'

'But it's possible that it is in the future too?'

'Yes, you are right.'

'All right, so M. is a writer, right?'

'Yes, he is a writer.'

'Very well then; either he wrote this story, or we will have to write it in his head so he writes it at the exact time, right?' said the Devil.

'Yes, you are totally right. I must say that it's either a coincidence or a new wormhole will be open. That sort of energy is out of our control. What do you think this means, Devil?' God took a better look at the old oak tree. The oak tree was dead; dried, greyish. The branches and the leaves and everything about it were dried dead, but it didn't crack; it was petrified; waiting for a touch. 'And this with the numbers; it's crazy, don't you think? And this tree is waiting for water, is it not?'

'Yes, you are right,' said the Devil. 'So, for when will we have to plan this? Do you want me to kill him for you?' asked the Devil.

God gave it some thought and said: 'We can pin it on Cruz.'

'Oh yes, you are right; let's send a virus with the artefacts. It's a good idea, easy. Let's bring them to us. When do you want to make that happen?' asked the Devil.

'Well, I can make it happen now. But I'm worried about the Virgin, my wife, and my son; Cruz can go fuck himself. It was him who projected this shit when he read the book. He lost his faith and allowed a singularity.'

Mary was lost. She was watching her husband deciding something, but she couldn't know what they were saying. 'Fuck. Fuck this shit! This shit can't be happening; not to me. I have been waiting for 2,000 years!' Mary was crying in silence like a baby. Jesus; poor guy was still high and Father Cruz had shit himself; beautiful.

God was looking at that picture and was thinking with the Devil: 'Why; why the fuck did I allow intelligence?'

'Well, it's not like you allowed anything, was it?'

'What do you mean? Ah, OK; natural selection? That matter.'

'Yes, that matter; so, did you plan everything in your head?'

'Naturally, why do you think I have been so quiet?' answered God.

'Hello? You don't have your hat. I have been listening to everything all along.'

'Of course, you have,' patronised God. 'I think we should tell them something.'

'I agree. It's your flock, so it's only fair you doing the honours.'

'Naturally,' said God with his mind somewhere else.

'Chill out. This is just a pause in our game. Nothing will change, right?'

God didn't answer. Before he talked with them about how there would be repercussions for their acts, God briefed them with his plan of discovering why M. and A. both had to be there in that day and how that would be the only possible way of putting an end to that tree and that third door. 'The tree is here. The reason why is because of you, Cruz, and you will be the one hosting those two once they cross the portal and also the one with the task of taking him to the tree.'

Mary opened her eyes by double and in silence, looking at Cruz, she walked slowly towards God who took her under his arm like a chicken does with a little chick. God had a cock expression. The Devil was laughing inside, and Jesus wasn't quite sure about what to do. Jesus was tired of praying. He was tired of voices of people crying and asking forgiveness. Everyone gets tired at some point. Let's give Jesus a break; after 2,000 years it's only fair to allow the man a middle-life-crisis. Why don't, instead of praying in his name, why don't we start praying in the name of our real fathers and our children, our friends and why not a little prayer for our enemies too? I'm sure they appreciate that. God carried on: 'When you read the book you believed in something better than Heaven, Cruz. When you did that, because you are in holy unstable grounds, you projected what you envisioned, and you created the tree and this path. You know me well, Cruz. You know how fair I am with my flock, but what you did has no forgiveness. For that I'll offer you only two options: either you managed to cross this door – but we have seen already what happened to those over there,' and he pointed to the other saint, the demon and the monkeys, all still unconscious on the floor, 'or you will go with my friend the Devil.'

'Oh, thanks, mate,' commented the Devil. God breathed deeply and gave a bit more thought about everything. Then he looked at the Devil.

'What do you think? Let's do this shit?'

'Yes, sure, can't wait.'

'Fair enough,' answered God and talked to Cruz. 'Cruz, you go the entrance of the portal and wait.' Cruz was ashamed and embarrassed. He walked slowly the 50 feet separating the portal and the place where the path had turned in two. If God had asked him to go brush himself with shit and go look for flies, I'm sure he would do it. 'Stop there! It's enough!' ordered God. Cruz stopped facing the portal door. 'OK, here we go.' God closed his eyes and Heaven started shaking and their shapes blurred and trembled. Nothing happened. God did it again; nothing.

The Devil opened his eyes and asked: 'What's going on, why are their souls not obeying? Why is their twist so irregular?'

'I don't know, damn it! You know what to do, do you want to try?' answered God insecure.

'By all means, my friend; it will be a pleasure.' And the devil tried to sink M. and A.'s rotation and bring them through the portal; nothing; nothing happened.

'It feels like we can't read them; can you read their presence?' asked God slightly confused.

'Nope; nothing; either they lost their souls, or they can actually avoid our presence. You don't think they can read our minds, do you?' asked the Devil with a smile on his face. 'Chill out, my friend. Maybe it's just the way it is. Is this not the first time you try bringing two at the same time through the portal? Everything is fine; maybe they got lost inside the portal, ahaha.'

The Devil was always trying to cheer up God but he wasn't in the mood for jokes. 'And what about this fucking tree? This is their story. Only those two can sort out this shit! If they disappear, this fucking story will never end!'

'Yes, my husband is right. Whatever this is, we need to put an end to it,' declared Mary in a more lucid way. Her fears had disappeared once she touched her husband. She was feeling more confident. 'Come on, who the fuck would cause any troubles to God? Only a strong message would ridicule Heaven or its inhabitants, but even that would not be good for everyone. Where would the magic go? Where would people's hope go? God is the creator of all things and the only omnipotent being in the Universe, let's not forget about that.'Mary reinforced her message looking at the Devil like he was the only gay in town.

'I'm not going to bother answering you that, Mary, because of His presence, but things might not be as straightforward as you think…the symbolism of their numbers and the fact that we are fusing them so they can cross the portal might be a totally new game we are playing here. Moreover, we both commanded them to cross the portal, and nothing happened yet, and that is already a new start for us…' answered the Devil in a very introspective manner. The water-like wall covering the portal passage started moving intensely. The initial lake-like stillness gave way to a river-like one.

'What's happening; why is the portal doing this?' asked Father Cruz from the distance.

'I don't know. You stay exactly where you are, Father,' replied God disguising his astonishment with the behaviour of the portal passage that should always be still and only slightly affected during the quick moment of crossing. Someone should have crossed it, but no one could be seen for now. Everyone started feeling uncomfortable and agitated. The portal door was now screening what seemed like a tropical storm. Cruz closed his eyes and started praying. God, the Devil and the Virgin walked a few feet closer to Cruz while Jesus was checking on the monkeys and the other two still fallen unconscious on the floor near the old oak tree. Strong winds started shaking the other trees leading to Heaven and Hell. The sky got grey, and suddenly everything stopped, and the wind stopped and the skies turned blue again. They all looked at the portal coming from the Limbo and nothing again.

CHAPTER 18

Judgment day

'Ah, what is this? It feels so good,' thought M. while twist-ing. M. and A. were now at the portal accessing the Limbo but they couldn't see each other yet. Their twist slowed down until it stopped, leaving them back to back with mil-lions of souls trying to push their way through the queues closer to the portal. From there they would cross through Limbo and after; Gate of Destiny. 'Ohm, what the hell is this?' M. twisted, stopped facing the portal and A. stopped too facing the same direction; M. look bored and then he looked at his father and saw him. He smiled. 'Father? How nice of you being here with me.'

'It's been a while, kiddo.' They both faced the portal and walked through the portal.

'Ah, this is nice, perfect. What do you think? Fish-ing, and playing football. What do you think?' asked A.

'I think this is amazing!'

'Calm down, M., please? Let's just pretend it's not happening; let's calm down.'

'Can you feel it?' said M. enthusiastic.

'It's nice to be here with you again. I'm sorry that it took me so long finding you. Being here now with you makes all the difference.'

There was a moment of silence.

'We are not dead, Father. How is this possible?' A. was quiet.

'M., it's time,' declared A. 'We need to go. Let's say our numbers.'

'You know that I might transform once I go through the portal.'

'Naturally. That's why I'm here with you. It doesn't matter any more, you wrote this shit and what can we do now, M.? This is happening at the exact time line we need to get us there.'

'We need to find a way,' said M. 'We need to be able to come back as we move forward. Do you know what I mean?'

'Yes, like momentum. I understand what you are saying and now just say the fucking number, please, M.'

'8. – 5. – . 13.'

'Do you think this shit will take long?' asked the Devil.

'This is stupid. I'm getting annoyed that I have to be here now, but I can't let this tree be here, I don't feel well with it in here,' said God.

'I know what you mean. How do you think he is going to look like? Have you?'

'Yes, of course I have. I've been here since the beginning. I know everything because I created everything, are we clear about that?' God was losing it.

'I never told you that I really like the things you write, my son. I had your book with me when I died in Africa. I threw it away somewhere in the jungle hoping it would seed. It did. Someone up there got interested with your book, M.' A. was lecturing M. as they crossed the portal to Heaven. Outside God and the Devil were marking the tree when the oak tree came to life and from there M. and A. came out. 'Hey, you cocksucker!' said A. to the Devil. The oak tree was shining. M. and A.'s shapes of energy were projecting like sun into God and everyone else.

M. said, 'I'm tired of this shit!' His voiced echoed like thunder for a few moments. 'Why do you care?' M. asked all of them. 'Why do you even bother?'

God and the Devil were still a bit sceptical. The Virgin Mary had fainted. Father Cruz was having a chat with A. 'It looks like Father Cruz was my father's human God,' said M. looking at God.

'Yes, it does. A lot of this story makes a lot of sense in the particular world. Did you read my mind?' asked God to M.

'Yes, I did, you cocksucker, and so what? Now you are going to cry or are we going to play some games, huh? Do you see this door behind me?' asked M. to one of them. No one was really in the mood to talk much. Everyone was a little bit surprised. I guess that was because they were thinking that door would lead to another magical place above. It was nothing like that.

'And why did you have to kill me?' asked M. to God. God wasn't scared. God was worried.

'What's going on, God? What are you thinking about? How will we play this?' The Devil was talking with God in his thoughts until M. asked God in his mind:

'He is a bit stupid, isn't he?' God did not answer.

'Nice suit,' said M. inside the Devil's head.

'You cocksucker!' said the Devil. 'You stupid thing. Stay in your corner.' M.'s energy extended and contracted like a baby spring as slowly as butterflies in the summer. There was a new energy in the upper world. M. and A. are up in space. God was distressed and he was tired.

'OK. So, you are here, and now what? What do you want?'

'Excuse me? What do I want; you need to stop playing your little games of the mind shit, because you were the one that fucking killed me. You think you can do it again?' M. wanted to fight God.

'M., no! If it comes to it, I'll do it, OK? Please, M., we are here now and look: Father Cruz; God, the Devil, the Virgin Mary and a few more lying on the floor...'

'No, Father! This needs to be done and these two here will have to help us.' M. was so confident. The scene was so fucking slow. 'Listen, God!; my father wouldn't mind being the gatekeeper of this new door we opened here today, you can set up a members' card or something like that, sit them down in front of a TV watching their life like it's a movie, but the souls need to be judged and the ones that are good are not even given to the Devil. M. spoke and said again: 'Oh, and I and my father will have one door each leading to our own after world.' M. said this, closed his eyes and the entrance for the three gates changed and two other doors were created. M.'s was made of steel and

A.'s was made of wood. Many more stories will happen to those few in the upper world and maybe I will be here to tell them or maybe not, or perhaps next time I'll talk about the story of Oliwia and I.

AUTHOR
ACKNOWLEDGMENTS

I would like to thank my family and friends and to all the letters of the alphabet that supported cared and always believed in me.

Thank you to LR Price publications for all the effort put in publishing this book. Thank you to the Managing Editor, Russell Spencer for all your patient and supportive words throughout the process.

Finally a special thank you to my friend Oliwia Lis, without whom this story would have been probably forgotten in the files of my computer.

Thank you all and enjoy your reading. I'll see you in my next fiction.

Marco

ABOUT THE AUTHOR

Marco Paulo Da Silva Dias was born on 3 March 1976, in Caldas da Rainha Portugal

In 1996 he went to Law School. He graduated In 2002 Modern Languages and Modern Literature at the University of Lisbon. Later in 2002 he graduates in Marketing and Multimedia at the Portuguese Catholic University.

During his years of university he initiated writing poetry and published some of his poems at the city local newspaper.

In 2009, Marco publishes in Portugal and in Portuguese language his first 2 poetry works – ***O Livro das horas Vagas*'** and later in the same year, ***Humildade e Presuncão'.***

In 2011 Marco wins an International competition for both Portuguese and Spanish languages held in Brazil. His chronicle Somos tudo não sendo nada' is then published in São Paulo Brazil - collectanea *Nocturnus'*.

2020 marks the year starts his adventure in the English language and Oliwia is his first published fiction.

Marco moved to England on 31 December 2012 and lives in Brighton since then.

ABOUT THE PUBLISHER

L.R. Price Publications is dedicated to publishing books by unknown authors.

We use a mixture of both traditional and modern publishing options to bring our authors' words to the wider world.

We print, publish, distribute and market books in a variety of formats including paper and hardback, electronic books, digital audio books and online.

If you are an author interested in getting your book published, or a book retailer interested in selling our books, please contact us. www.lrpricepublications.com

L.R. Price Publications Ltd,
27 Old Gloucester Street,
London, WC1N 3AX.
020 3051 9572
publishing@lrprice.com